The Hidden Tomb

Kate felt a strong sensation. Not a voice; nothing so definite. More of a beat inside her head, a drum beat, a throb of blood. Then a rushing sound, like the inside of a seashell. Then the cold, clammy feel of a rising tide, as if the garden was awash, as if the lake was rising to drown the house. She felt she was sinking in a cold tide; then a whisper of leaves, or voices, drifted through the air.

"This way!" Kate gasped. She knew, she just knew where to find him!

For Christine Dodd

Hippo Ghost

The Hidden Tomb

Jenny Oldfield

Scholastic Children's Books
7–9 Pratt Street, London NW1 0AE, UK
a division of Scholastic Publications Ltd
London ~ New York ~ Toronto ~ Sydney ~ Auckland

First published by Scholastic Children's Books, 1995
Copyright © Jenny Oldfield, 1995

ISBN 0 590 55799 8

Typeset by TW Typesetting, Midsomer Norton, Avon

Printed by Cox & Wyman Ltd, Reading, Berks.

10 9 8 7 6 5 4 3 2 1

Chapter 1

Everyone said the old man was mad. He was wild and ragged, and lived alone in the woods.

"Leave him," Lucy said. "He looks like the sort of person we shouldn't go near." She went on unloading rough wooden stakes from the trailer.

But Kate stopped work to watch him walk by the lakeside. She could see why they called him mad. He muttered as he walked, staring down at the ground. He was stooped and thin. His clothes were torn, his hair was wild and white.

"Where's he going?" Lucy whispered. He walked deep into the woods.

"Home, probably," Kate said. She watched the thin, dark figure disappear into the shadow of the trees. "Todd says he lives somewhere in there."

"But there's no road!" Lucy said. "Not even a proper track. Where's the house?"

An impatient voice interrupted them. "Isn't anyone going to take this heavy fence post from me?" Todd demanded. "Or am I going to do all this work myself!"

Kate and Lucy grinned and went to help. Soon they were caught up again in carrying posts, digging holes and clearing the undergrowth for the new footpath. They worked in the sun and fresh air, feeling good to be doing something so useful. Soon they forgot the old man.

"Right, that's it for the day!" Dave, their leader, called at last.

Everyone straightened their aching backs

and heaved a sigh of relief. Kate went and chucked her spade on the trailer. Conservation work was great, and she was glad she'd volunteered for the National Parks spring project in Middleton Wood, but she hadn't expected it to be this tough. Still, "Race you for the shower!" she told Lucy. She went on ahead, forcing her tired legs into a run.

She thought of what had brought her here to this out of the way village; how her parents' developing computer business had taken them abroad for the year, and how she'd come to stay with relatives so she could carry on at school in nearby Hedley. Todd's mum was her mother's cousin. Staying with them had worked out really well. It had been a wrench when her parents left, but now she'd settled in and was enjoying country life.

The path she'd taken led down to the water's edge, then up a gritty slope between the trees. Sun still dappled the ground and shimmered gold on the water, but the shadows were longer. Evening drew in.

"Wait for me!" Lucy shouted. "Kate, where are you?"

With a smile, Kate decided on a trick. She took a detour; a side path somewhere near where the old man had disappeared into the woods, she remembered. Quickly she ducked down and hid.

"Kate!" It was Lucy's voice again, bubbly and excited. Lucy had been her friend since first school, and for this week of half term holiday she'd been allowed to come up to the farm to stay.

Kate heard footsteps coming closer. She crouched lower in the bushes.

"Oh, I'm going! I'll get back to the farm before you and have first shower!" Lucy said in a loud, obvious way. Kate heard the footsteps retreat. She decided to leave her hiding place and cut across country through the woods, to beat Lucy back to the farm. She was tall and quick, with a good sense of direction. She reckoned she could easily do it.

So Kate set off, nimbly dodging through the blossoming blackberry bushes. She skirted patches of nettles and headed deeper between the trees.

The wood smelt damp, even on this sunny day. Soon everywhere was in shadow, but she kept going, keeping her bearings, alert to all sounds and movement.

Rabbits bobbed and darted down their burrows. A large bird clattered from the branch of a tree high into the air. Kate saw it was a magpie. "One for sorrow," she thought, remembering the rhyme. But she ran easily on.

In a clearing, deep in the woods, she came to a sudden stop. There was a house; here, miles from anywhere. And she'd never seen anything like it!

It stood in what had once been a garden. A broken-down wall and a screen of thorn bushes almost hid it from view, but there were tall chimneys and part of a stone roof visible. It was definitely a house. Quietly Kate crept nearer to the crumbling stone gateposts. The garden was nothing but brambles and over-grown grassy mounds. In one corner some old apple trees stood bent and twisted. But the house itself – that was really amazing!

Kate thought it must have been here since the beginning of time. A massive place, built of huge stone blocks turned mossy green with age. Its roof sloped and dipped in all direc-tions. The tiny windows were partly boarded up. The great arched entrance was choked with ivy. But there was one room at ground level where the window panes were still intact, and inside that room a bare electric lightbulb shone. "Someone still lives here!" Kate breathed.

It could only be the mad old man, she knew. Yet still, when he flung open the ivy-choked door and came stamping down the path towards her, shock seized her. She cowered back behind the gatepost.

"No, no!" he muttered savagely. He stopped in the wilderness of thorns.

In the silence that followed, Kate risked another look. The old man was bent far forward. His hands were clutched to the sides of his head. They shook with terror.

"No, no!" he groaned. "Not this time!"

Kate felt her heart moved with pity. Such sadness. Such suffering. If he was mad she was sure he was harmless. His white hair flew back from his face in a sudden breeze, but his lined face, sharp as a bird's, stayed in shadow. Still he groaned and sobbed and muttered.

Bravely Kate stepped forward. No longer frightened, but anxious for him in his fit of pain, she went slowly towards him. "Can I do anything?" she asked.

The old man looked up without seeing her. "No, no!" he said, looking beyond her.

Kate turned round. There was nothing there, only the trees sighing in the breeze.

"Do you need anything?" she said. "Can I help?" He looked so thin and frail that it seemed the least thing could defeat him. His hands shook as he drew them up to his sharp, shadowed face.

"Again!" he moaned. He kept his hands clutched to his head, horrified. Still he ignored her, except for one split second when he glanced up, seemed to see her and shake his head.

Then, shaking, almost staggering, he turned back up the path.

Slowly Kate followed. She watched him pause to gather strength at the carved stone entrance. He leaned against the door. After a few moments he went back into the dark, cold house. The door slammed. The electric light in the ground floor window burned on.

Kate stared. She felt drained and helpless. Poor old man. She went on through the woods.

When she got back to Highfield Farm, Lucy

was already showered and changed. She teased Kate. "So much for trying to trick me!" she laughed. "Did you take a wrong turning?"

Kate nodded. She looked at herself in the bathroom mirror; thick dark hair down to her shoulders, wide mouth serious at the moment, dark-lashed brown eyes. How could people get so lonely and sad as that old man; so tired and careworn?

"Come on," Lucy said gently, changing her tone. "Time to go and eat." She could see something had happened to Kate. Maybe she'd tell her about it over supper.

"Oh, that must have been old Oliver Mason again!" Todd overheard Kate describing what had happened in the woods. "I told you about him when you first arrived, remember? Top of the list of things and people to avoid in Middleton!" He was only half joking.

"I didn't know that was his name." Kate

had got her appetite back and was tucking into a hefty pile of mashed potato. With Todd filling her in on the old man's story she relaxed and her mind cleared.

"He's lived there all his life, just like all his family before him." Todd settled in for a chat, elbows on the table. He'd begun to find life much more interesting since Kate had come to stay with them at the farm. He'd lived here all his life and helped out as much as possible. Now, with Kate in residence and Lucy staying, even clearing plates and washing up dishes began to look like a halfway decent occupation. "They say the old place is in quite a state now," he added.

"It is. Parts of it are all boarded up. One wing has nearly fallen down. The roof's collapsed at any rate." Kate had just finished describing her meeting with the sad old man.

"Hardly anyone goes near," Todd admitted. For as long as he could remember, people in the village had gossiped and told all sorts of wild stories about the old house in the woods. But he never recalled anyone actually going near the place. "People just leave him alone to get on with it."

"Get on with what?" Kate shook her head and looked at Todd. He was acting as if leaving a poor old man to fend for himself in a deserted place like that was a normal thing to do. If it was up to her, she'd be doing something practical; meals on wheels, shopping. She'd be getting involved. "Why?" she asked. "Why doesn't anyone go near?"

Todd looked awkward. "Don't know. I think maybe people tried to help him keep the place together at one time. It's not as if they don't care. But that's just the way it is." He shrugged. "No one likes going down to the Hall, that's all."

"The Hall?" Kate asked. Her view of the old place had fired her romantic imagination. She liked mysterious houses with hidden secrets.

"It's Middleton Hall. That's what they call the place." Todd answered, but he found himself wanting to change the subject. The youth club was on down in the village tonight. He wanted Lucy and Kate to come along.

Lucy looked at Kate with raised eyebrows. "It sounds very grand: Middleton Hall," she said.

"It was once, I reckon. The biggest house around. But I'm talking about a long time ago. The Mason family had pots of money then. They must have had, to build a place like that," Todd fiddled with the food on his plate and looked thoughtful.

As he talked, Kate pictured the tumbledown house set in its wild garden. But yes, it must once have been grand. She remembered the stone carving over the door, and a date inscribed there in old fashioned numbers: 1634.

"Anyway," Todd said. He stood up and did his best to sound casual. "Anyone fancy coming down to the youth club tonight?"

"Yes!" Lucy said like a shot. The outdoor life suited her. The sun had already put extra blonde lights in her long hair and turned her skin golden brown. She jumped at the chance to chat and listen to music. She went straight off to get changed.

"OK," Kate agreed. Chat and music weren't so much in her line. If she was honest, she preferred a good book; a mystery or a romance. Still, she didn't mind joining in.

"Great!" Todd said. He especially wanted her to come along. He liked the straight way she talked about things and her no-nonsense, sleeves-rolled-up manner. She'd settled in really well since her mum and dad went off, and she'd really got stuck in to the conservation work this week, digging a ditch, shifting stones with the best of them. He'd watched her.

Kate's eyes narrowed. She scraped the remains of her pudding from the plate. "On one condition," she teased.

Todd laughed and folded his arms. "What's that?"

"If you tell me why they call you Todd? It's your family name; the Todds of Highfield Farm!" The nickname had puzzled her for years.

She'd worked it out; Todd must be her second cousin or something like that. She'd marked him down as the strong silent type. He was tall, dark, a bit moody whenever she'd seen him at family gatherings like weddings and Christmases. He seemed fond of going off into a corner by himself. But now she was living here, she'd warmed to him. He gave her straight answers and always meant what he said. Now she felt easy enough in his company even to tease him lightly. "Go on, how come you're just Todd and nothing else?" she insisted.

He shuffled uncomfortably. "I never liked my first name, that's why!"

"Why not? What is it?" Kate hopped up

and sat on the pine table, almost nose to nose with Todd. She had a teasing grin on her face.

"Heslington," he muttered. Wow, this was embarrassing!

Kate's mouth fell open. "Heslington! I've never even heard of it!" she said. "Is it a real name? Heslington Todd!"

"You see!" he said, feeling hot. Then he shrugged. "Now you've got to come to the youth club!"

"OK!" she said with a cheeky grin. She jumped down from the table. "Meet you in ten minutes!" She ran off to join Lucy, upstairs getting ready.

The quick route on foot into the village took them down from Highfield Farm through the wood and along by the lake.

An evening quiet held sway. There was no wind now, and all the rich flower scents wafted in the air. Lucy walked up ahead, eager to get there. Todd walked behind with Kate.

"Look at the sun on the lake!" she said, stopping to gaze at it. "It's red and gold. It's unbelievable!" Lucy drifted on.

"We'd best catch up," Todd reminded Kate. He saw two figures walking towards them from the opposite direction. It was Mick and Tez, two kids from school. He gave a wave and saw them stop to greet Lucy.

Kate sighed and looked around. Of course, this was where the path split off and one part led up to the Hall. The old, overgrown track was unforgettable. "Maybe we could just drop in quickly on old Mr Mason?" she suggested. She couldn't forget the terrified look on his sharp, birdlike face.

"You can't just 'drop in' on the Hall!" Todd protested. There were those weird stories about it that he'd avoided telling her. Besides, it was getting dark. "Let's catch up with Lucy!"

Kate held on to his arm. "Please!" Something seemed to draw her up the old path, something stronger than curiosity. She was a girl who followed her feelings through and who liked to help. She went on ahead, hoping Todd would follow. But she was going to see Mr Mason anyway. She had to check to see if he was all right. It left Todd with no choice but to follow.

"Hey!" he said. He caught up with Kate at the old gateposts. The old iron gates were long gone, the path up to the house almost grassed over. He thought at first that no one could possibly live here.

But the light still burned in the downstairs room. "Come on!" Kate said. She marched up to the door and knocked.

They held their breaths. Inside, footsteps slowly shuffled across the hall, and even more hesitantly the door creaked open.

Everything lay in deep shadow. The first thing Kate made out was the old man's shock of white hair, then his hand trembling on the door handle. He looked puzzled. "Who's there?" he said.

Todd took in old Mr Mason's terrible state; his tattered jacket all coming away at the seams, his collarless shirt. "Don't worry, it's just two of us from Highfield Farm, Mr Mason," he said. "We thought we'd drop by to see if you needed anything." The old man looked thin and ill, but calm enough. There was no moaning and groaning now, and he certainly didn't look mad.

He shook his head. "Nothing, thank you." Even his voice sounded rusty from disuse. He stood there peering out at them like some old caged bird. His eyes glittered in the last, low rays of sunlight.

"Then can we help you with anything?" Kate insisted. She was relieved to see that he'd calmed down since this afternoon. But surely there was a job they could do for him, an errand they could run?

The old man cleared his throat. "There is, there is," he said quickly, as if making a big decision. He beckoned them in as he shuffled ahead across the dark, stone flagged hall. Taken aback, Kate and Todd tried not to stare at the primitive conditions; doors off their hinges, ashes piled high in the huge open fireplace, the smell of damp wood and soot. They followed through into the kitchen.

Here a single bare lightbulb glared down from the cracked ceiling. There was a huge table, an old wooden dresser, another open fireplace and a careless stack of wood. The cooker was an old, grey iron thing on claw feet. Big iron pots hung from hooks sunk into giant oak beams which stretched the width of the room. Everywhere was covered in a dark film of dusty grease.

But the poor old man seemed at least to be making one last effort to make the place decent. On the table in the middle of the room was a stack of old paint tins and some big, stiff looking brushes. He'd already started on one wall, trying to cover the flaking grey plaster with a fresh coat of white paint.

He pointed at the table in irritation. "Can't open the tins," he muttered. "Too old, too weak, hands too shaky!" He held them up for Todd and Kate to see. They looked like old, gnarled claws.

Was this all it was? Todd gave Kate a grin. "No problem!" he said. His face broke into a friendly smile.

Kate went quickly and found a strong old knife in the drawer in the table. She handed it to Todd, who began to lever off one of the rusty lids. A strong, sharp smell of paint hit the damp air.

"It looks as if it's still OK," she told Mr Mason. "It just needs a stir." She went to the hearth and picked a long, straight stick from the pile of firewood.

The old man nodded. "I wouldn't normally trouble you," he apologized. "Only I must get this job done quickly!" He came and peered at the paint.

Kate stirred it. "We'll help!" she said

brightly. After all, he was nearly helpless, his hands trembled so much. And between them she and Todd could slap on a coat of paint in no time. She seized one of the grimy old brushes.

Todd flashed her an impatient look, but he could hardly refuse. He took up a brush and headed for the dirtiest, flakiest old wall, the one by the door.

"No, no!" the old man said sharply.

Kate and Todd turned to look.

"This one, this one! We have to be quick!" He pointed to the opposite wall. His voice had become a low hiss.

"But you've already…!" Kate began. But she broke off in dismay.

Mr Mason's hands had gone up to his head again. He was shaking it in disbelief.

"What is it? What's wrong?" Kate asked. It seemed as if the room had suddenly gone dark. One last strong ray of light filtered through the tall trees of Middleton Wood. It pierced the gloom in Mr Mason's kitchen, caught him standing in its beam. It shone a gloomy red on the old man's face and hands.

"No, no!" he whispered in that dreadful hollow voice.

"What's wrong with him?" Todd asked. He dropped his brush and backed off towards the door.

"It's the same thing as before," Kate warned. She moved a step or two towards the old man.

But he saw nothing, no one. His breathing came fast and shallow. Still he stared at his clawlike hands. "The voices!" he said, so low and faint they could hardly make it out. "Hear the voices!" He held his hands to his head in total horror.

"What, Mr Mason?" Kate pleaded. "There's nothing! Please don't do that!"

But the old man pointed into the gloom. He pointed at nothing. "The voices! Stop them! Stop them! Can you hear?" he cried.

"They're arguing, listen! Oh no!" He dropped on to his hands and knees as if to stem a tide, making wild, sweeping motions across the floor.

"What's he doing? I can't hear anything!" Todd yelled. In his own horror he thought the air had suddenly turned icy cold.

Kate felt it too; there were no voices, but a cold wind swept through the room. She backed towards Todd and clung on to his arm. "Mr Mason, please stop it!" she cried. "There's nothing here! Please don't do that!"

The old man rose from his knees. He threw back his head like a drowning man. His arms flailed, his hands clawed, but it seemed he was sinking. "No!" he pleaded. Something bubbled in his throat, choking him. "No more!" He staggered from the room. He clutched his throat. He gasped for air out in the tangled garden.

White blossom floated, ghostly in the gloom. Kate and Todd kept their horrified distance.

"Stay back!" Todd warned.

But Kate rushed towards Mr Mason to help. She saw him whirl towards her and stagger forward. She felt the blank, dead stare of his glinting eyes. The claws of his hands reached out to catch her by the neck. Just in time she fell sideways from his grasp.

Todd ran and caught hold of her. "Let's get out of here!" he gasped. He grabbed her arm, pulled her up and started to run with her to the gate. The wood yawned dark and thick ahead of them.

Kate took one last look. The old man was slumped against the doorway now. He moaned and clutched both hands to his head, frantically shaking it. He was sobbing.

"Let's go!" Todd insisted. "The old chap's mad, didn't I tell you! He doesn't need us. Let's go!" He dragged Kate on.

The house melted into the gloom. The thorn bushes swallowed it from sight. She was so afraid that she turned and ran. "It's haunted, isn't it?" She gasped out the words as they ran on to the main path. She was breathless, her hair straggled in wet strands across her face. She pushed it back. "The Hall is haunted!" She stood face to face with Todd.

"They say it is. But I don't believe that stuff!" he said fiercely. "He's crazy, you hear!" And he stormed off towards the village.

"Don't go talking about ghosts and all that rubbish!" he insisted as they went into the youth club. "I've heard the stories until I'm sick of them. People round here who believe them need their own heads looking at! There's no such thing, you hear!"

Kate gasped at his anger and struggled hard to make herself act normally. Todd was in a foul mood over it. "OK, I won't mention it!" she promised.

"Good!" He stared back over his shoulder. "Because I don't believe a single word of it, OK! And there's no point talking about it! He's just one mad old man, that's all!"

Chapter 2

Inside the youth club everything seemed normal. It was light and noisy, and with Lucy around no one could stay serious for long.

She came straight up to Kate. "What kept you?" she asked, bright and bubbly.

Kate looked at Todd. "Nothing really."

"Oh-ho, 'nothing really'!" Lucy giggled. "We know what that means!" She linked arms with Kate and took her up to the bar which served soft drinks. "You sure you're OK?" she asked. She handed Kate an orange juice. "You looked really pale when you came in."

Kate smiled. A few people she knew from

school wandered across, Mick and Tez amongst them. Mick was Todd's mate at school. He was always telling jokes, and Todd said he sent all the girls wild with his sleek dark hair and tanned complexion. Tez wasn't so flashy looking; he was quieter and shyer. His family ran the village store. Kate liked him better. She'd seen him delivering groceries round Middleton on his bike.

Lucy studied Kate's serious face. "I bet you sneaked up to the Hall again, didn't you?" She gave her a dig with her elbow. "You could have given me a shout!" Kate might have known Lucy would want to see it for herself.

"You never!" Mick's face went into a shock-horror expression. "Hey, Tez! Kate and Todd just paid a visit to the ghost house!"

Soon everyone was crowded round to hear the story.

Todd glowered at Kate and leaned moodily against the wall.

"You're not serious!" Mick went on, even though he could see he was annoying Todd. "You visited the Hall! Did you see any ghosts?"

"Stop it, we don't want to talk about it," Todd said through gritted teeth. "Of course I know all the stupid stories about a ghost haunting the Hall; who doesn't around here?" But, as he'd told Kate, he refused even to start to believe it.

"Did *you*?" Mick asked Kate. "You know the old place is haunted?"

Kate recalled the old man's wild, drowning struggle and his cries about the voices. Even now, she could feel that cold, clammy sensation on her skin. But you didn't talk about ghosts in the clear light of day. Or rather, in the bright lights of a youth club. And anyway, Todd had warned her not to. So she just gave Mick a little push and told him to stop fooling around.

"Take no notice," Tez said quietly. "I've

been up there loads of times myself, and I never saw a ghost."

"You've been up to the Hall?" Lucy took him up. "How come?"

"I take stuff up to the old man. Groceries and stuff. I usually dump them on the door-step for him. And I never saw anything daft like a ghost."

"Oh!" Lucy couldn't help sounding dis-appointed.

"No. He's just a bit peculiar, that's all. He's harmless, though."

Others chipped in with their opinions. "*You*'d be a bit peculiar if you lived up there all alone for the whole of your life!" someone said.

"Tez is peculiar anyway!" Mick cut it.

Soon everyone was joining in the laughing and joking.

Later, though, when Todd, Lucy and Kate walked up the road to Highfield, they gave the walk through the woods a miss.

"Let's take the main road," Todd said. "It's too dark for the path."

No one argued. They sang loud songs and kept close together. Twenty minutes later, they were all safe in bed, and Kate's memory of the strange, demented old man was already beginning to fade.

It was Lucy, with her own lively imaginings, who renewed the subject at breakfast. "Mrs Todd," she said as she joined her in the farm–house kitchen, "I want to know the whole story about Middleton Hall! Everyone joked about it at the youth club last night, but they wouldn't tell us. There *is* a story, isn't there?"

Todd's mother flicked over rashers of bacon in the enormous frying pan. She was a plump, cosy woman who smiled and chatted easily. But she was too busy to talk right then.

"You certainly choose your time!" she said. She went on cracking eggs and spooning hot fat over them. "Why don't you ask Todd?

He's sitting at the table like a spare part, doing nothing!" She flipped a tea towel off her shoulder and in his direction.

Todd was in fact sitting with Kate, tucking into a big breakfast.

"OK," Lucy said. She liked local gossip and was determined to get to the bottom of this.

"It has something to do with two brothers falling out. Something to do with who owned the house," Mrs Todd said. "Todd knows all about it. He studied it for his local history project." And she carried on with her cooking, humming as she worked.

Lucy nodded and went to sit down. She asked him straight. "Todd, what's this about a feud between two brothers at Middleton Hall?" She cut neatly into her bacon and looked him in the eye.

Kate stopped in mid-mouthful, her attention immediately drawn. Todd could also see Lucy meant business. And this morning, a bright, breezy one, the events of last night were easier to shake off. He'd been scared, he had to admit. But now there was no reason he shouldn't pass the time telling them the story of the brothers' feud. After all, he did know the facts. He waited while Lucy settled down. He could reel it off without having to believe a single word.

"It's true, there's a terrible curse on the house!" he said. He made his voice echo and tremble.

"What sort of curse?" Lucy asked. Here he was, fooling around just like Mick last night.

"A curse on anyone who owns it! A curse on the whole Mason family!" He made ghost noises. There was no way he was going to take this seriously.

"Go on," Kate said. That meant the old man was cursed, then. But what was the curse?

"Once upon a time!" Todd said.

"No, seriously; go on!" Kate insisted.

"Lucy wants to know."

"And I suppose you don't?" Lucy said.

"OK, I want to know too," she confessed. "So get on with it, Todd!"

"Right." At last he dropped the funny stuff. "The house was built in the seventeenth century by two brothers. Both brothers belonged to a family of stone masons who built all the farm houses round here. By the time they inherited the business, they'd made enough money to build a big place of their own."

"Middleton Hall?" Lucy asked eagerly.

"Hang on!" Todd said, grinning. "So they chose a place by the lake and began to build. Everything was fine until they started to argue over who would inherit the place after they both died. Apparently, the older brother, James, claimed it was his because he was the firstborn, and the oldest always had most rights. The younger brother, Oliver, didn't like that, naturally enough."

"Oliver?" Kate cut in. "That's old Mr Mason's name, isn't it?"

Todd nodded. "The whole family seems to have been called Joseph, or James, or Oliver. I looked it up in the parish records."

Kate looked hard at Todd. He must have taken his history project pretty seriously, to go to those lengths. In fact, he sounded like an expert on the Mason family. "Go on!" she said.

"Well, anyway, the story goes they had a massive fight over the house even before it was finished. And on the night of the fight the older one, James, disappeared. He was never seen again!"

"Murdered?" Lucy's round, sunny face went deadly serious. "That's awful!"

"Nobody knows. Of course, everybody said Oliver had murdered James, but they never found a body. They searched the woods, the lake, everywhere. But they couldn't prove a thing!"

"So what happened?" Kate asked. She'd stopped eating and gave it her full attention.

"So Oliver was left to finish the Hall. It was the biggest and best for miles around. He should have been the happiest man in the county!"

"But?" Kate prompted.

Todd sighed. "But according to the legend, Oliver hadn't lived in the house a month before he sent everyone away – wife, children, servants, the lot. He refused to see anyone. He just ranted around the place, shouting and moaning."

"What did he shout?" Kate whispered. The story had her in its grip. She was beginning to shiver.

Todd gave her a sharp look. "How should I know? I wasn't there."

"Doesn't the legend tell you that bit?" Lucy asked.

Todd stood up. He'd had enough. "No, all I know is that this Oliver brother went mad.

35

And that a lot of the family has been mad too, right down through the generations for hundreds of years!"

"Wow!" Lucy shook her head in disbelief.

"And now old Mr Mason's mad!" Kate concluded.

"He must have inherited it!" Lucy said.

"Well, you wanted to know," Todd said moodily. He began to move off. "See you down at the site," he added. The volunteers had to gather each day at nine. He wondered what was the matter with him. He wasn't usually this short-tempered.

"And that's the curse of Middleton Hall!" Lucy declared. "People who live there go mad!"

"But why?" Kate said. They took their plates to Mrs Todd at the sink. "Thanks," she said with a vague smile.

"Did Todd tell you what you wanted to know?" Mrs Todd asked Lucy.

She nodded.

"That Middleton Hall has been a sad place by all accounts." Mrs Todd said she didn't know the ins and outs of it. People always talked, it was true. "Even when I was a little girl they said we shouldn't go near the old place. My brothers used to frighten the life out of me, telling me about ghosts down there. Scared me to death!" She laughed. Anyway, she just knew she could never stand living like that old man up at the Hall. Not that she believed in ghosts and curses nowadays. Not really. People generally made their own luck in life. "Now the old place is just about ready to fall down, I hear. And maybe it wouldn't be such a bad thing!" she said. "Get the old man into a home where he can be properly cared for." She wiped her hands on the tea towel and said a cheery goodbye.

Kate and Lucy went out into the yard. "Hi-ho!" Lucy said, shouldering her shovel. She'd heard enough gloomy stories for one day, she decided. "And off to work we go!"

"What?" Kate nearly bumped into her as Lucy adjusted her stride.

"The seven dwarfs!" She ordered Kate to fall into line and in step; "I'm Happy. Which one are you?"

"Grumpy!" Kate said, frowning. The stories about Middleton Hall were bothering her more and more.

But Lucy always cheered her up and they both went off laughing.

Kate and Lucy realized that they'd volunteered for a week of hard work rebuilding the path. But it felt like a good change to be doing something useful out of doors, and a week wasn't a long time to give up. After this, it would be schoolwork as usual.

They worked hard right through the day. A new stretch of path had to be levelled and packed down. They supported it at one side with wooden stakes and long, shallow boards, to stop it crumbling away. Dave, the leader, came along every so often to position the stakes and offer advice. Then he went on to the next little group.

When they broke for lunch, the girls sat on a grassy bank eating sandwiches and quenching their thirst with bottled water. Then a figure they recognized came cycling up. "It's Tez!" Todd waved to him from the water's edge. Tez slowed down. "Where are you off to?" Todd yelled.

"To the Hall, to drop these things off." Tez grinned shyly at Kate and Lucy. He pointed to a box of groceries fastened securely to the back rack of his bike. "Do any of you lot fancy walking up there with me?"

Todd shrugged and began to back off. He mumbled something about finishing his lunch. But Lucy jumped up. "I'll come!" she said. "I really want to see this place!"

Todd's eyes widened. "Are you sure, after what I just told you?"

But she ignored him, and joined Tez.

Kate looked across at Todd. "Coming?" she asked. "Maybe we ought to check that he's OK? The old man, I mean."

"We're not his keepers," Todd objected. But try as he might to resist, he couldn't help feeling involved after yesterday. So he scrambled up the path and cut ahead of the others. "As long as we're quick!"

"Don't be long, you lot!" Dave yelled from his sunny spot by the lake.

"Fifteen minutes!" Kate called. They took the half-hidden track, helping Tez to take the big cardboard box from his bike and carry it between them.

The house stood, green with moss, crumbling with age, as it had stood yesterday and for the last three hundred years. Kate gave Lucy a second to get used to the idea that anyone could still live here, then they followed the boys up the garden path.

"Spooky!" Lucy said. She tilted her head for a better view of the ancient stonework, the missing slates and broken chimneypots. "Look at all that ivy!"

"The door's open!" Kate said.

"That's funny!" Tez put one foot inside. "He usually keeps it locked."

"Call him," Kate suggested. It was strange to leave the old door creaking in the breeze like that. "See if you can make him hear."

"No, just leave it on the doorstep as usual," Todd suggested. His nerves were all on edge, remembering their last view of the old man standing here in this spot, dragging his hands down his chest and moaning. Lucy and Tez hadn't seen that. They didn't know what they might be letting themselves in for.

But Tez ignored him. "Mr Mason!" he shouted. It echoed in the stone hall. There was no reply. Tez walked further into the house.

"Look at the size of those old beams!" Lucy had followed him inside. The house was everything she'd imagined; cobwebby, dark, full of nooks and crannies. The windows were too narrow to let in much light and some were even boarded up. There was a carved wooden staircase winding upstairs, and across the hall an entrance into another room. "This must be the kitchen," she said, and stepped inside.

Her shout echoed through the whole house. Kate heard it from outside and ran from sun into shadow. Still Lucy's yell pierced the air. Kate followed the sound. She heard Todd follow her.

In the kitchen they found Lucy, pointing to the wall. Her shouts had died down and turned to jerky sobs.

"It's all right. It's all right," Kate said gently. But Lucy pointed.

Tez, who'd come in last, saw it first. He followed Lucy's pointing finger towards the far wall, the white wall. It didn't look white any longer. The rough plaster surface seemed to be daubed and smeared with dark patches. The blotches made some sort of pattern.

"What is it?' Tez asked. He felt as if he'd walked into a nightmare. It felt damp in here, and the whole wall was a mess. "Is it just marks, or letters, or what?"

Gradually Lucy stopped sobbing. Kate went up closer to the wall, but the shapes were even more blurred. It looked as if it was still wet, whatever it was. She put out a finger to touch a patch. It was sticky. "What is it?' she gasped.

Lucy groaned again. "It's disgusting!" she said. She clung on to Kate.

"Calm down. We can wash it off!" Todd protested. He felt sickened, and turned and went outside.

Tez stared.

Kate stood and traced the shadowy shapes on the white wall. "It's a word!" she said. "This is a 'T'! It begins with a 'T'!"

"Don't be daft!" Tez argued. He tried to think. "If it's a letter, what's it say?"

They turned and stared at him. There was no answer they could think of.

"Well!" he protested." Where's the 'T' in this first bit?" He felt himself beginning to panic.

Kate stared down. Her fingers were stained dark brown from the damp patches.

"Come away," Tez told them. Kate shielded her friend's face from the dreadful wall and led her outside.

"That's the wall the old man went on about," Kate told Tez. "Todd didn't want me to mention it, but Mr Mason kept on saying that was the wall we had to paint."

Tez nodded. "We'd better try to find him then!" He sounded grim but determined. "The trouble is, he could be anywhere!"

"But not here!" Kate looked all round the kitchen. Her eyes were drawn back to the wall. They were letters, she was sure. Smeared letters made by shaking fingers. If only she could read what it said! But she swayed and felt faint. Turning, she saw that Tez and Lucy had already gone. She staggered against the table. The old paint tins rattled. A half open one tipped and spilled. The white paint oozed onto the table, dribbled through cracks and began to drip in great white splashes onto the dark stone floor. Kate fled outside.

"Did you find him?" Lucy asked. She was feeling better out in the fresh air.

They all waited for Kate to answer. She closed her eyes, waited for the trees to stop whirling overhead. Then a thought struck her. "The door was open!"

"Yes?" Todd told himself to get a grip. "So?"

"Yesterday, when he started that nightmare thing inside the house, and all that crying and moaning, he made for the garden, didn't he?"

Todd nodded. He remembered how old Mason had run out, eyes glinting, black jacket flapping like a terrible ragged crow.

"So, it's the same today!" Kate said. "He's run for the fresh air and left the door open!"

Tez looked round wildly. "He could still be anywhere!"

But Kate felt a strong sensation. Not a voice; nothing so definite. More of a beat inside her head, a drum beat, a throb of blood. Then a rushing sound, like the inside of a seashell. Then the cold, clammy feel of a rising tide, as if the garden was awash, as if the lake was rising to drown the house. She felt she was sinking in a cold tide; then a whisper of leaves, or voices, drifted through the air.

"This way!" Kate gasped. She knew, she just knew where to find him!

They struggled after her through thorn bushes. She felt them catch and tear at her bare skin. They followed Kate down to the old apple trees and found her bent over a hunched, lifeless shape under the trees.

Apple blossom had drifted like confetti onto the black, threadbare jacket. The white hair spread around the lined, shrivelled face. The eyes stared black and wide.

But it was the hands that horrified. Clutched tight to either side of his head, they were like sharp claws trying to shut out those dreadful voices.

Kate listened to the whispering leaves. "Vengeance!" they seemed to cry, far off and ghostly. "Why, brother, I shall have vengeance!"

Chapter 3

Kate and Todd stayed with Mr Mason while Tez and Lucy ran for help. Of course, there was no hope, nothing they could do.

"He's been dead ages," Kate said. Yet the sun still shone, the birds still soared overhead, as if nothing was wrong.

Todd sat on the grass at her side, well away from the body. "You think it's got something to do with this curse, don't you?" he said miserably.

Kate nodded. "Didn't you feel it? Out here

in the garden. There was a pounding, rushing sound. And what about the voices?"

Todd was forced to think about it. "I never wanted to believe in that," he said. "When I had to do that work for school I thought it was just a load of superstitious rubbish. Not real."

"And what do you think now?" Kate stared at the old man's corpse.

Todd was even slower to answer this time. "I don't know. Maybe." How else had he died, if not from ghosts and curses? "But maybe he just believed in that stuff himself. It all just went on inside his head, you know? But it got so strong it literally frightened him to death."

"What about the voices?" Kate whispered. "Did you hear them?" She wished Todd would explain it to her. She wanted some reasons.

They sat in silence and waited.

* * *

Even the police had to admit it was strange. They took him away in an ambulance, the men in white tunics running up the path with a stretcher. A few policemen had taken photographs, examined the area and asked questions. "We're not treating the death as suspicious," they told Mr Todd when they came up to the farm that evening. He'd taken charge once Tez and Lucy had come running up from the Hall with the dreadful news.

"You're not?" Mr Todd waited for more information. He held up his hand, warning them not to interrupt. They all sat at the kitchen table, still shocked and shaken.

"No, there's no reason to," the police inspector said. "The doctor says he died from natural causes; a heart attack."

Mr Todd nodded slowly. "What about the other circumstances?" He was a practical man with a steady voice and a broad build; just right to cope with emergencies. Even when Todd had described the letters daubed on the wall, he took it calmly, called the police and said they must wait and see.

The Inspector looked puzzled. "Other circumstances?" He looked from one to the other in the crowded farm kitchen.

"The letters on the wall, voices Mr Mason heard!" Kate said. She felt herself grip the table.

"Now steady on," the policeman said. He cleared his throat in embarrassment. "We got a report about that, and my men responded. We looked for evidence of violence on the body." He paused awkwardly.

"We did see it!" Kate said, feeling the doubts creep in. She could see that the policeman didn't believe them, so she looked round at the others.

Their pale faces bore witness to the grim facts. "Yes, we did!" Lucy agreed. "There was a mess all over one wall!"

But this time the inspector shook his head. He looked at Mr Todd and beckoned him into a far corner of the room. "It looks to me as if they're all suffering from some kind of shock, sir," he said quietly. "When we arrived on the scene there was no sign of all these letters they'd been talking about."

"Kate, sitting safely in the warmth of the Todds' kitchen, couldn't believe what she'd just heard. They'd seen and heard it; the weird brown pattern on the wall, the whispering voices that drove the old man mad.

"I think possibly they were a bit hysterical, having found the body like that." The inspector went on advising Todd's dad. "Just keep them quiet, let them talk it through, keep an eye on them, all right?" He took his hat from underneath his arm and fixed it firmly on his head.

Mr Todd nodded. He looked puzzled, but he shook the inspector's hand.

"You have to believe us!" Kate cried. She stood up and felt Todd try to hold her back. "No! We saw it! It's the curse of the Hall! It came and got the old man! He didn't die of a heart attack! The curse came and got him!"

Even as she spoke, she felt her voice falter. When she finished she sat down again at the table, feeling weak and useless. She knew how ridiculous it sounded.

The inspector's face gave nothing away as he watched Lucy go up to Kate and comfort her. Then he turned to Mr Todd for a final word. "As I said, sir, we gave the whole place a thorough going over and we're satisfied that no one else is involved in the old man's death. There's nothing missing from the house as far as we know." He gave a faint smile. "Not that there was anything to steal! And as far as the corpse was concerned – no violence, no marks on the body." End of story! he seemed to be saying. He nodded slightly and let Mr Todd show him to the door.

"Don't worry, Inspector, I'll make sure that things calm down here," Todd's father told him.

"Yes, please, sir. It's best not to encourage these stories in the neighbourhood. There's bound to be enough talk as it is." He sighed. "It doesn't help anyone; least of all the poor old chap himself!"

Mr Todd nodded in agreement. He closed the door as the policeman went out.

Inside the kitchen there was a stunned silence. What did they do now? The four of them looked at each other in total confusion.

"So what happened?" Tez whispered. "Who washed all the blood off?"

"Not me!" Kate said.

Lucy and Todd both shook their heads.

"Someone must have!" Kate insisted. Their voice were low whispers.

Mr Todd was looking unhappily at them, uncomfortable with this latest development. He would just have to follow the inspector's advice – wait for the shock to wear off and let them get back to normal.

"It couldn't just disappear!" Lucy agreed,

still shaken by the memory of discovering the ghastly rusty red graffiti trickling down the wall in old Mr Mason's kitchen.

Todd sprang up from the table. "We don't know that," he said, his face grim. "Maybe it could!"

"Disappear!" Kate echoed. "What do you mean?"

But Todd wanted to be outside, away from all this. He felt stifled. "I'm saying maybe it could disappear, once the old man was dead. Maybe that's what the curse involves. It's the ghost giving us a clue of some sort!" He paused. "On the other hand, maybe we're all crazy!" He made for the door.

"Todd!" Kate called out. "We saw it!"

He turned. "We think we did!" he said. Then he slammed the door and vanished into the dusk.

Lucy was the first to speak. "He's wrong!" she said, her clear face full of trouble.

Mr Todd came across. "Maybe. But no

crime, no police action," he said. "You heard."

"But what if it was the curse?" she said.

He sighed. "Even it it was, what do you want to do, arrest a ghost?"

Kate was still silent. Todd's remark had felt like a terrible betrayal. And she grieved for the old man, knowing how alone in the world he'd been. "What happens now?" she said at last.

"Who knows?" Mr Todd began more briskly. "But I agree with the inspector that you need time to get over the shock. Don't worry about Todd; I'll go and find him. Then I'll drive you home, Tez." He smiled at the girls. "How about an early night for you two?" he suggested.

Wearily they let themselves be organized. It had been the worst day of their lives, they freely admitted. They'd be glad when it was over.

* * *

Most of Middleton village came to Oliver Mason's funeral. The little square church was packed with people wanting to pay their last respects.

They gathered in the churchyard afterwards to shake their heads sadly in memory of the tormented old man, and perhaps to wish they'd done more to help when he was alive. They wondered about his death. Rumours had spread. Half of the people there nodded wisely after the event and said that they'd known all along that the curse of Middleton Hall was a thing to be reckoned with. "My grandmother knew old James Mason way back, before the last war," someone said. "And the same thing happened to him. The old chap went on and on about voices in his head, and nobody knew what to make of it. And then they found him dead just like this!"

The rest shrugged and said no, they didn't believe it. Superstitious nonsense! Just like

Todd, Kate thought. She listened to the village gossip, her own mind in a whirl.

But soon they got on with life; farming the hills, tending their gardens, meeting in the pub. Within a few days things were back to normal. The old man might never have existed.

"Mrs Todd, do you think Mr Mason died of natural causes?" Kate asked. She'd offered to help with the washing up after supper. It was three days after they'd found the body, and time was bringing no answers. Todd still refused to talk about the mystery of the vanishing letters. She had to discuss it with someone.

Mrs Todd sniffed and sank a pile of dirty plates into the foamy water. "Use that cloth over there," she said.

"Well?" Kate knew that even Mrs Todd didn't like to talk about it, but thoughts were jammed inside her head, locked in, jostling one another. What happened to the letters? was the one that got most in the way.

"Yes, I do!" Mrs Todd said stubbornly. "Heart attack, wasn't it?" She looked Kate directly in the eye. "That's what the doctor said, and as far as I'm concerned, that's it!"

"But there was a word written in something that could have been blood on the wall!" Kate cried.

Mrs Todd nearly bit her head off. "I don't know about that!" she snapped. "But I do know he's dead and gone, poor old man. And now I think you should just let him rest in peace!" Then she sighed. "I'm sorry," she said. "I didn't mean to be so sharp. It's just that I don't know what to think myself."

Kate sighed and dried the dishes. What about the word? And what did those voices say? she asked herself over and over again. But no one was giving her any answers.

There was never any chance to go back and find out for herself, even if she'd managed to pluck up courage to return.

Work on the footpath had to be finished by the end of the school holiday, then Lucy moved out of the farm, back home to Hedley. The next week, Kate found herself almost relieved to be back at school, back in routine. Lessons, homework, letters to her mum and dad, visits to the youth club; these were the things that took up her time. Spring blossom gave way to flowering hedgerows and the hay-gathering of high summer.

They got on with life and let the haunting memories fade.

So it was almost out of the blue when Lucy came up to the farm one evening and burst into Kate's bedroom with an announcement.

"Did you hear, someone's moving in!" she exploded with the startling news.

Kate looked up from the book she was reading. "Moving in where?"

"Into the Hall!" Lucy clambered on to the top bunk. "Todd says they've half moved in already! The dad and the furniture came today. The mum and two kids are moving in tomorrow!"

"You can't move in there, it's falling down!" Even Kate's romantic imagination fell short. "Who is this family?"

"Ask Todd," Lucy spread her palms, "if you don't believe me!"

So Kate jumped down and went straight and did just that. She eventually found Todd out in the field at the back of the farmyard. He stood, arms resting on the stone wall, watching the herd of black and white cows quietly grazing. It was dusk. The cows looked flat, like cardboard cutouts, against the emerald grass.

"Who's moving into the Hall?" she asked, not wanting to beat about the bush. She leant against the wall beside him.

"The old man's nephew," he told her without looking round. "Jim Mason, and his wife and two kids."

"Don't they know?" she said in an awed voice.

"Know what?" Todd said sharply. He sounded like his mother. If this was another of Kate's attempts to talk about the old man's death, he didn't want to know.

"About it being haunted!" Kate said, but her voice trailed off. She could see she'd annoyed him again.

"No, they don't. No one knew about Jim Mason before now. I think he's from some distant branch of the family. Until they had to sort out Oliver Mason's will, no one even knew he had a nephew. And I doubt whether the nephew knew about some crazy old uncle hidden away in the back of beyond. It must come as a bombshell to find out you've got family you never even heard of!" He turned to look steadily at Kate. "And if it turns out they haven't heard any of these stories about the place, there'll be no point you telling them, will there?" he said.

"Why not?"

"Because it's not true!" he said angrily.

He'd moved away from believing all that rubbish since he'd sat with Kate watching over the corpse. The police had sorted it all out and that was that. He looked away at the horizon. "That was just a load of superstition. Remember what the inspector said!"

She swallowed hard, then changed the subject. "But what about the state of the place?" she asked. "Do they know it's practically a ruin?"

Todd's voice softened. "They do now." He was sorry he'd hurt her feelings. "My Dad met up with Jim Mason in the village today. They got talking. My Dad said to him, 'That's some job you've taken on up there! Just give me a shout if you ever want a hand with anything.'"

"And?" Kate prompted. She was beginning to realize after a few months of living with them that you had to stick to practical things when talking to the Todds.

"Jim Mason thanked him. He'd realized the

old place was a mess. But he's out of work at present. They had to sell up and move, so when he did get the news out of the blue that he'd inherited this place from an uncle he'd never even heard of, he grabbed it with both hands. 'I was never afraid of hard work,' he told my Dad. My Dad said, 'No, that's just as well, then.' Jim Mason thinks he'll be able to knock it back into shape; he worked as a builder before he went bust."

Kate listened carefully. She was curious to meet this Jim Mason, she had to admit. "It sounds like a fresh start," she said.

Todd nodded. "It is. And they've been down on their luck, so don't go putting them off with any silly stories, OK?"

"OK," she agreed. Like the people of Middleton, she was nearly ready to get on with life. Some questions just stayed un-answered, she thought. And that would have to be that.

Chapter Four

Work at school and on the farm continued, while work on the Hall began. A builder's skip arrived, pulled by the Todds' tractor over high fields above Middleton Woods. It drove down a narrow farm track between the trees. When Kate set off for school each morning, she would hear the sound of hammering echo down the hillside. Jim Mason was up and already busy.

Sometimes she saw him to wave to; a stocky man in his forties with wavy, greying hair. He always had a cheerful greeting for anyone passing by, but he was always stuck into his work, shovelling rubble or mixing concrete. Kate guessed he would be popular; a friendly, easy-going man with lots of guts and determination.

And Kate and Lucy both decided straight away that they liked the look of the Mason kids too, as they cycled into school.

Nick was about their age, with the same wavy brown hair as his dad, and his easy-going smile. He wore baggy clothes that always looked crumpled and too big. Sophie didn't look so cheerful. She was a bit younger; about twelve, they guessed. She had a serious, pointed face and light brown hair which she wore tied back in a pony tail.

"No wonder she's fed up!" Lucy said. "Fancy having to put up with all that mess!"

They watched her ride towards the bike shed, her bike loaded with her school bag.

"And changing school, leaving all her friends and everything," Kate agreed. It meant everything to her that she hadn't had to do that when she came to stay with the Todds.

"Let's ask her to come along to the youth club," Lucy suggested.

So they decided to go over to the Hall after school.

The track was still overgrown, and trees still shadowed the clearing where the Hall stood, so that Kate shivered with the memory of poor Mr Mason. But the house itself had begun to change beyond belief. There was builder's rubble everywhere; plaster and stone heaped into the skip, neat piles of stone set by ready for rebuilding. Ladders and scaffolding ran up the front of the house, and Jim Mason himself, in jeans and a red checked shirt, scrambled nimbly across the sagging, uneven roof. He waved and called down, "Nick, Sophie, you've got visitors!"

The children came out of the open front door, followed by Todd. With a huge hammer in his hand and plaster dust in his hair, Todd looked as if he'd already made himself useful.

"Grab a chisel!" he yelled. "Don't just stand there!"

"What are *you* doing here?" Kate demanded. He certainly didn't waste any time.

"Lending a hand. We're chipping away at the damp plaster, getting back to the stone."

Kate knew he'd just finished a day at school. Didn't he ever need a break? "We came to see if you want to come out tonight," she told Sophie.

Sophie dipped her head shyly and hesitated.

"Course you do, Soph!" Nick said, giving her a shove.

"Are you going?" she asked him.

He nodded.

Sophie looked up at the two girls. "OK, thanks," she said.

Mrs Mason came out at the sound of new voices. She was a slight woman, and not much taller than Sophie. Her hair was covered by a red patterned scarf and she was dressed in dark green men's overalls with a red belt pulled tight around the waist. She looked kind of artistic and interesting, Kate thought, as she sat on one of the piles of stones.

"They've asked me to go out with them tonight," Sophie told her with a pleased smile.

"That's nice." Mrs Mason pulled the scarf off her head and let her brown hair hang down to her shoulders. Clouds of dust rose as she brushed herself down. "Give me 6H any day!" she moaned.

"Mum's a teacher," Nick explained. "Or she was, before we moved."

"Other people spend their evenings lounging around watching television or playing sport!" She gazed round at the building site they called home. Then she looked up at her husband still scrambling about on the roof. "Go on, Jim, tell me again that it's a challenge!" she called. She sounded tired but amused. "Tell me how wonderful it will all be when it's finished!"

"It'll be peaceful and beautiful, with real log fires in the inglenook fireplaces. The garden will be full of flowers and apple trees. No one will disturb us and the sun will shine every single day!" he replied with a grin that was so infectious that soon everyone was smiling with him. "It'll be brilliant! Is that what you wanted to hear? Now, someone please pass me that crowbar lying in the grass down there!"

Nick grabbed it and scooted up a ladder.

"Be careful, Nick!" Mrs Mason warned. "It's chaos!" she said to the girls. "Will somebody tell me what we've let ourselves in for."

Kate smiled uncomfortably. If only you knew! she thought. Little flickers of memory had been set alight by Mrs Mason's innocent phrase.

But Todd gave her a warning look. "Are you two going to lend a hand?" he said. "Or just stand around doing nothing."

Lucy grinned. "Give me that hammer. Tell me where to start!"

Soon they'd formed a work gang inside the house. They cleared old plaster from the kitchen floor and wheeled it out in barrows as Nick, Todd and Francine Mason chiselled it off the ancient stone walls.

"Home sweet home!" Jim called in as he passed through the hall, trundling a wheelbarrow full of rubble before him.

"It's good to have new blood in the village," Mrs Todd was saying to Tez's mother. She'd bought sliced loaves and Kate was ferrying them out to the Land Rover. Work had been going on at the Hall for over a week now, during the long, fine days of mid-July. "I hear they're making quite a difference up there," she said.

Mrs Hebden agreed. "Yes, though I don't envy them the job they've taken on."

Mrs Todd piled more loaves on to Kate.

"No, but Jim Mason works until he drops. He's a good sort. And luckily he's come in from the outside, so none of this family curse nonsense should prey on his mind."

"What about her?" Mrs Hebden liked to be up to date on people and events, so she could pass things on to her customers.

"Francine Mason? She's pretty quiet, keeps to herself. She's a hard worker, like her husband."

"But not so keen on the move, I hear?"

Mrs Todd considered this. "Well, would you be? There's no proper cooker, no hot water, nothing!" They all knew how the old man had lived. "It's not an ideal spot to bring up a family. Not that they had any choice. The Hall came as a godsend, with them going bust and losing their own place."

"Needs must," Mrs Hebden agreed. "Still, I don't envy them." She shook her head across the counter at Mrs Todd.

Todd's mother paid for the loaves and went

with Kate out to the car. They set off up the hill.

"Would you drop me here, please?" Kate asked as they drove by the side of the woods.

Mrs Todd slowed down. "Are you off to the Hall again? You and Todd seem to be down there every spare minute these days!" she said.

Kate nodded. They were keen to help the Masons in their struggle, and Todd kept showing her up by getting there first.

"You're not mentioning anything unpleasant, I hope?" Mrs Todd leaned across and spoke through the open window as Kate jumped down onto the grass verge.

"No," Kate said quickly. "I haven't breathed a word!" She agreed it was best to say nothing. She would just go to work, help and forget about the ghost, or whatever it was that had terrified the old man.

Mrs Todd put the Land Rover back into gear. "Good!" she revved the engine.

"They've enough on their plates without worrying about what happened to the old uncle." And she drove off up the hill towards the farm.

It was Saturday, a day off from school and homework for Kate. The day, which had begun clear, had turned grey and cloudy. A thunderstorm threatened and Kate wondered whether Lucy would wait at home in Hedley until it had passed. She pressed on up the path. Anyway, she'd be working indoors, finally helping to get the kitchen straight.

Sure enough, the electric light glared and she spotted figures crossing the narrow window. She went in without knocking. In the kitchen, Jim was scraping away at the last remnants of plaster still clinging to the wall opposite, while Francine scrubbed the stone flags on the floor. The white emulsion paint spilt by Kate on that dreadful day was coming off fairly easily. Todd was up a ladder. He tapped nails into new plasterboard which he'd fitted between the giant oak beams. There was no sign of Nick and Sophie.

Kate set to work scrubbing down the old table.

"It should come up nicely," Jim said. "Give it plenty of elbow grease!" He stood back for a moment and gave her one of his warm smiles. "We really do appreciate this," he told her. "Everyone round here has been fantastic!"

She smiled back. "We're glad you came," she answered. "And I think the Hall is really lucky to get such a nice family!"

Carried along on their wave of enthusiasm, she was truly beginning to believe that the curse, or whatever it was, had been beaten. With the walls stripped bare, and the crumbling sections of the house under repair, it definitely felt as if Jim Mason and his family could settle in here and live a normal life.

For a while they worked quietly. It began to rain heavily; huge spots driving against the window pane in the wind that had just got up. Inside, the noise of a chisel chipping away, hammers hammering, brushes scrubbing filled the silence.

Then suddenly Jim stopped work. "That's odd!" he said. He put his fingertips to the bare stone wall.

"What?" Francine glanced up.

"Nothing," he said. He shook his head. But he ran his broad hand along the surface of the wall and stared at it, mystified.

Kate watched him put his hand gingerly to his nose and sniff. She tried to keep calm. It's nothing! she told herself. Stay cool! But she felt Todd stiffen too. She glanced at the wall. There was nothing to see.

"Huh!" Jim stopped again and stood right back. He stared down at his hands.

"For goodness' sake!" Francine sighed. "Will you stop making those grunting sounds!"

"No, that's definitely odd!" Jim went back and put both palms against the rough surface.

"Come over here. Can anyone feel this damp patch? Just here. It's sticky!"

Kate and Todd inched forward. They dreaded his next words.

"I can't feel anything," Francine said. "It feels dry as a bone to me!"

"No, here!" Jim insisted. "And here!"

They could see him getting more excited. Nothing upset Jim Mason. He was always easy going and happy. Now his face looked startled. He jerked his head, seeking some explanation for what he'd felt. "Can you see anything dark down here?" he asked. "Todd? Kate? Anything sticky and dark?"

"No." Todd said, truthfully. To him the wall looked clear. But his voice sounded hollow.

"No!" Kate said. Her own voice was faint. Just when she'd pictured a happy life at the Hall, here it was beginning all over again!

"It was seeping through the stone!" Jim insisted. He looked closely at his hands, then back at the wall. "It's gone now, anyway."

Kate breathed again. Todd cleared his throat and climbed his ladder.

Francine went back to work. "It's not like you. You must be overworking!" she said.

"What isn't like me?" Jim began to sweep up a pile of plaster.

"This imagining things. And having night-mares like the one last night."

Kate stared down at the circular soapy patterns she'd made with the brush on the wooden surface. She felt afraid of what was coming next.

"Oh that! That was nothing!" Jim shrugged it off. "It's not even worth mentioning. I wish I'd never told you!"

His wife frowned at him. "So you say!" she said. "But I think there's more to this than meets the eye!" She turned away. "He had this dream," Francine told them. "Something to do with a dead body. It had been hidden and Jim said he had to find it. It was one of those dreams where you run down dark corridors and you're looking for something and you can never find it. Anyway, he woke me up. He was sitting bolt upright in bed muttering something about voices. He stared round the room saying, 'Where did all these voices come from?' It took me ages to calm him down!"

Kate had nearly stopped breathing. Todd froze at the top of the ladder. All their worst fears were coming to light.

"We're all working too hard!" Jim declared with an uneasy laugh. He chucked down his brush and slapped himself down with the palms of his hands. "Down tools, everyone!" He grabbed Francine by the hand. "I'm taking you out for a meal!" he said. "Come on, you two, that's enough for today!" He sounded his normal, cheerful self.

So they said goodbye, and Kate and Todd set off through the woods and across the fields to the farm. It had stopped raining. The thunderstorm had never arrived.

Kate ran beside Todd. "You heard him!" she whispered. They were in the middle of a field without a soul in sight, but still she whispered.

Todd nodded. "I heard."

"He saw patches on that wall!"

Todd ran on grimly, his mouth tight shut.

"And he had a dream about a body and voices everywhere!"

They ran towards the horizon, where bruised blue clouds met the dark land.

He nodded again.

"How could Jim have heard about the curse?" she said, desperate and afraid. "No one has breathed a single word!"

"How should I know?" Todd said savagely.

Kate stopped and caught him by the arm. She had to make him listen. "Todd, that house really is haunted!"

"We don't know that!" he protested.

"Yes, we do! There's a curse on it, and it's haunted!" Her voice seemed to echo against the empty hillside. "And, Todd, we know what really happened to Oliver Mason! The curse did get him! And now it's getting Jim! The whole thing is beginning to happen all over again!"

Chapter 5

Kate and Todd watched each event at the Hall with mounting fear. They would try to kid themselves that things would work out, and yet day by day they dreaded something terrible.

"Jim's different from the rest of the Mason family," Todd tried to tell Kate. They were walking together from Highfield down to the Hall, drawn to the place each evening after school, yet afraid of what they might find. "Jim's an everyday sort of bloke, just like my Dad or anyone else in the village. He won't let himself be beaten by some old story!"

Kate nodded. She wanted to believe it. "I know what you mean." She looked up through the branches as they entered the wood. Banks of gold and white clouds drifted overhead. It felt calm; a million miles away from bloody scenes of death and destruction. "I agree; if anyone can get through this it's Jim Mason!"

Yet the other, more fearful half of herself had to admit the changes that were overtaking the new family at Middleton Hall.

She still joined in the work with a will, but she saw that Jim was growing to be a shadow of his cheerful, lively self. His face was drawn and grey, he stopped whistling and bustling about the place. Instead, he went quietly, half-stooped, fixing his mind on this roof beam, that chimney stack, as if this was the only way to stave off the nightmare. "I must get on," he said whenever Kate, Lucy, or Todd visited. "You don't mind if I don't stop for a chat, do you?" It was all so different from when he'd first arrived.

"He never even breaks off to eat," Nick complained. He showed Todd and Kate the outline of what might be a doorway in one of the downstairs rooms. It had been bricked up, but Jim wanted it all opened up again. Nick had discovered that the wall was thick and would take a lot of work to knock through. "I don't think he stops to sleep either," he said. "He must be mad!"

"Don't say that!" Francine cut in sharply. She too looked thinner, more tired and anxious. Kate knew she'd always been less keen on the place, and now the strain was really beginning to tell.

"Just joking!" Nick protested.

"Well, it's not funny!" his mother said. "You father's taken on more than he can manage, that's all. And you should be doing all you can to help, not making fun of him like that!" She flashed him an angry look, then her face crumpled and she seemed about to dissolve into tears.

Nick mumbled, "Sorry," and shook his head as Francine went out into the hall. "It's like this all the time now," he confided. "Dad not talking, Mum shouting at everyone. Sophie just keeps out of the way up in the one corner of her room that's half fit to be in, poor kid!" He handed Todd a hammer and chisel. "I wish someone could explain what's happening round here!"

Kate opened her mouth to speak, but Todd's hammer hit the chisel a mighty blow and the ringing, rhythmical clash of metal on metal broke up the conversation. After that, she could only retreat and make herself useful somewhere else. Todd's furious hammering followed her out into the hallway and up the stairs. She went along a wood-panelled gallery towards Sophie's room.

Sophie was curled up in her window seat overlooking the old orchard, with the shimmering water of the lake just visible over the tips of the trees in Middleton Woods. She scarcely looked up as Kate went in.

"Hi!" Kate sat down on the bed. "I'm not interrupting anything special, am I?"

Sophie closed the book on her lap and stared out of the window. "No, I wasn't reading properly anyway." She sighed.

"It's hard to concentrate with so much going on around you, I expect?"

"No, it's not that." Sophie's voice was slow and quiet, as if half in a trance. But she was glad Kate had come up to talk. There was no one else who cared how she felt in this awful place. She turned and smiled sadly.

"What is it then?"

"It's this house! I hate it! Ever since we came here things have gone wrong!"

"It's bound to be strange at first," Kate said. She shifted uneasily on the bed. She wished there was something she could say to make Sophie feel better. The trouble was, everything Kate knew about the Hall would only make her feel worse!

"My Dad never had nightmares before we came here." Sophie protested. "Now he has them all the time! Anyway, my Mum says she can't stand it any more! Her nerves are all shattered and we've only lived her for a few weeks! She wants to take me to my aunty's house until the end of the summer holidays!" Sobs began to shake her body and her head hung forward.

Kate went over to give her a hug. She knew only too well how it felt when families had to split up for a while. "Well, maybe that's a good idea," she said. "Just until the mess is cleared up. But what about Nick?"

Sophie dried her eyes and shook her head. "He wants to stay here with Dad."

"And when will you and your mum go?" Kate helped Sophie pull herself together and tidy her hair. She brushed it back for her and put it up in her usual ponytail.

"Soon. She told Dad this morning."

"What did he say?"

Sophie paused. "Nothing. I don't think he really even heard what she said. I don't think he sees or hears anything any more. I don't think he cares about us, not since we came to this horrible house!" And she broke down again in Kate's arms, crying as if her heart would break.

At home, Kate and Todd could think of nothing else. They argued about it at mealtimes, to the point where Mrs Todd would cut in with an impatient reminder about homework or chores.

"You'd think nothing else mattered!" she complained. "And I'm sure you've both got plenty of schoolwork to finish before you break up for summer!" She looked anxiously across the lounge to where Kate stood at the door. "Kate, dear," she said more kindly, "I promised your mum and dad that I'd look after you properly and let them know if there was any trouble."

Kate nodded, ashamed of herself for worrying Mrs Todd.

"Well," she went on, "I've just about reached the point where I feel I ought to get in touch with them."

"Oh no!" Kate jumped in. "Don't do that. They'd only worry, and there's nothing wrong with me, honestly!" She tried to smile and reassure her.

"Then show me!" Mrs Todd settled back in her chair. "Try forgetting about Jim Mason for a change, and just give it a rest. If that house is proving too much for him, there's nothing you can do about it!"

Again Kate nodded. She backed out of the room. The voice of common sense told her that Todd's mum was right.

But still the problem would take her and shake her about like a rag doll. And she and Todd continued to fight over it in secret.

"What's the point?" Todd asked. They cut through the woods towards the Hall as usual.

"What's the point of telling them their home is haunted?"

"Then at least they'd understand what's happening to them!" Kate could have cried tears of frustration herself. "Instead of which, everyone thinks they're going mad and imagining things and having nightmares! And their family's falling apart for no good reason!"

Todd stopped to lean against the thick, rough trunk of an oak tree. He tilted his head to stare up at the canopy of emerald leaves.

"Why don't you want to tell them about the curse on the place?' she insisted.

He looked down at her. "Because even if they know, there's nothing anyone can do about it!" he said carefully, evenly. He'd thought this through many times.

"But at least you believe it now!" she said. "You believe there is a curse!"

"Yes," he admitted. He'd seen the haunted look in Jim Mason's eyes. He'd seen him washing his hands at the water tap in the yard, scrubbing and scrubbing at them until they were almost red raw. "Yes, there's a curse!" It hurt him to admit it because it turned his stomach with fear and made him feel weak and helpless again.

Kate nodded, satisfied. She turned and walked on down the slope. "Well, I don't believe there's nothing anyone can do!" she said. "I won't believe it!" Her voice was strong and determined.

"But it's existed for three hundred and fifty years!" Todd said. He ran to catch up with her. "They all hear these voices, see all the mysterious damp patches seep through walls and everything. Then they all go mad. And they all die." He stated it simply. How could you argue with a curse as old and strong as that?

Kate slowed down. They came out from under the trees, into the clearing where the Hall stood, half renovated, half ruined. "There must be something we can do!"

"What?"

"Think straight, for a start! It's got something to do with the story of the feud between those brothers," she reminded him.

"Everyone knows that!" he pointed out.

"I know everyone knows!" she frowned. She tried to get things clear. "But there's something about those brothers that we've missed!"

"Blood brothers!" Todd said gloomily. He felt scared and helpless.

Kate ignored him. "Something about them that we don't know. And when we know it we'll break the curse!" she said. That was it! They had to break it; somehow and soon!

"What? How?" Todd was having to run to keep up with her again. Then she stopped dead and turned in her tracks. She began to make her way back up towards the farm. Thank heavens that was still here, boring and normal as ever, Todd thought.

"I don't know what or how!" She came to

another sudden halt beneath the old hawthorn tree at the back of the farm. She put one arm around it and swung round to meet Todd face to face. "But curses can be broken, and we have to do it, OK?"

Todd nodded. "What about the others?"

"Lucy and Tez? They'll help too," she said confidently. From here on the ridge of the hill you could see miles in every direction; a patchwork of rolling fields, dark walls, heather and rock. "It's Friday tomorrow, isn't it? Let's arrange for everyone to meet at the bike shed!" she said. "Say four o'clock, straight after school."

"What for?" Todd strolled on ahead across the yard, hands in pockets.

"We're going to the library in Hedley." She watched his puzzled face. "To find a book," she explained.

"Yeh?"

"About Middleton Hall! To read about the legend, OK?"

"Yeh!" he nodded. "Good idea." At least it was a start. And when you felt this helpless and out of your depth, you needed a start!

" 'The Ghost of Middleton Hall'?" the librarian repeated with a puzzled frown. He wasn't sure what four sunburnt, high spirited kids wanted with a dusty book on local history. "Just a moment, please."

He went across to the computer screen to check the index.

"Maybe someone's borrowed it?" Lucy said. They stood at the high wooden counter trying to wait patiently.

Todd shook his head. "I doubt it. The last time I borrowed it, for my history project, no one else had borrowed it for at least a year and a half before that!"

"Not exactly number one on the bestseller list!" Tez agreed. He leaned on the counter and cast an eye around the old library; high ceilings, stained glass, millions and millions of printed words! "These places really get to me!" he said.

"Shh!" Lucy hissed. Two old men reading newspapers at a nearby table looked up.

At last the librarian came back. "Here's the title you want, and this is its classification." He handed a slip of paper to Kate. "I've written it down. You'll find it on the third shelf on your left, just past the photocopier." He watched carefully as the whole gang followed his pointing finger.

They found the right shelf. There was a whole row of maroon and brown books on local history: *Country Houses in and around Middleton, Victorian Middleton, A History of Middleton Woods.* At last Todd spotted the one they wanted. "Here it is!" He seized it from the shelf and they took it across to the reading section.

"*The Ghost of Middleton Hall!*" Tez read aloud in a spooky voice.

"Shh!" one of the old men warned.

So he lowered his voice to a dramatic whisper. " 'Chapter One'," he read. " 'Middleton Hall has been in the hands of the Mason family of Middleton since it was built in 1634. Originally a family of lowly stonemasons, they built many of the farms in the valley and over the years amassed enough money to begin constructing the ill-fated house in 1630.' " Tez looked up from the book. "Fascinating!" he hissed.

"We know all about that! Get onto the bit about the ghost!" Todd said.

Tez flicked forward a few pages. " 'Precise information about the fate of the missing brother has never come to light,' " he read.

"That's it!" Todd interrupted again. "I remember this bit. This is where it tells you about the ghost!"

" 'However, a legend quickly sprang up about circumstances surrounding his death. According to local tales, James Mason had been cruelly murdered by his younger brother, Oliver, in a dispute over the Hall. Oliver then disposed of the body by placing it in a secret tomb.' "

"A secret tomb?" Lucy whispered with a frightened glance at Kate. "Doesn't that sound awful!"

Kate nodded. "Go on!" she told Tez.

" 'Though many searches of the area were carried out, the hiding place was never discovered. Oliver denied the murder of his brother and took up residence at the Hall as soon as building work was complete. However, he was soon made to pay for his treacherous deed!' "

Tez paused to enjoy the serious faces crowded around.

"Go on!" Lucy said this time.

Tez read the next paragraph. " 'Within a month, it is said that he began to see visions and hear noises in every corridor and corner of the Hall and its garden. His wife and family soon left him and he shut himself up alone inside the magnificent house.

" 'Or was he alone? Local people who gained entry to satisfy their curiosity about the recluse reported hearing voices late one evening. The voices argued and cried out, but when they went to investigate, they found Oliver lying alone in his chamber, apparently scared out of his wits. They soon concluded that at least one of the voices they had heard was that of the dead brother, James.

" 'They later said that the ghost's voice promised revenge. It had told of being sealed in a great stone tomb where it suffocated and bled to death. It swore to haunt Oliver Mason and all his children. "And my blood will cry out 'Murder' in generations to come!" it cried.

" 'Witnesses at the scene wrote this down and swore it was true. Oliver Mason lived alone in the Hall for ten more years, but not one day of this time was happy. He died in 1644, crazed by visions of blood.' "

There was a long pause. "Is that it?" Lucy breathed.

"Nearly." Tez scanned the page. "It just says here that one expert may have noticed a pattern. Only the people in the Mason family who are named after the first two brothers, Oliver and James, were ever affected by the curse, and only if they decided to live in the house. And, listen, it says that only the victims can ever hear the voices and see the blood, right up to the time they die; then others can see it too, just for a few moments, before it fades away again."

"Yes!" Kate broke in. "That was true! The first time I saw old Mr Mason in his garden, he could hear the voices, but I couldn't hear a thing! I just thought he was mad. Then, when we found him next day, we could all hear them, remember? And there was all that stuff daubed over the wall!" She still shuddered at the memory.

"But by then it's too late. The victim always dies of heart failure; 'sheer terror', it says here." Tez read the last paragraph in a flat tone. He looked up uneasily.

There was a long pause. "Old Mr Mason was called Oliver," Kate said. No one spoke for a few seconds.

"But Jim Mason should be OK!" Lucy began. Then her jaw fell. "Oh no, Jim is short for James!"

The others nodded. Everyone was silent and serious. The old men at the next table went back to their reading.

Kate tried desperately to deal with the whirl of facts inside her head. She concentrated and waited until they settled, like snowflakes inside a paperweight. One question surfaced: where did the wicked Oliver bury the body of his elder brother? Nobody had ever found out. But the answer was vital. It might even be the clue they needed to break the old curse. And that was what she was determined to do!

Where? Where? She closed her eyes. 'A great stone tomb!' She could still hear Tez's voice reading out that chilling phrase. 'Sealed in a great stone tomb!' Tomb! The word had a dreadful sound. It rhymed with doom.

And then she thought of the pattern daubed on the kitchen wall. A scrawl, a desperate clue given by the ghost before the old man died? It began with a 'T'! She saw it again in her mind's eye as clearly as if she could really open her eyes and see it there. It began with a 'T' and it was divided into four sections. Four letters; 'T', followed by a rough circle, then a crude zig-zagging shape, and last of all a faint stroke and a curving line. 'TOMB'! It said 'TOMB'! The ghost had written it!

In his last breaths, choking and struggling against a host of invisible voices, with the curse upon him, the old man had been able to read the ghost's terrible clue!

"Kate, what's wrong?" Lucy asked. Her friend's face was pale and horrified.

"Mr Mason!" she whispered. "He knew the whole secret! Before he died, he saw the ghost's clue!"

"What?" Todd stepped forward. She whispered so low it was nearly impossible to hear.

"It was written down, but *we* couldn't see what it was telling us. It was a clue to the hidden tomb!"

Todd nodded. "It's OK," he said gently. "I get you." He looked around the group and led them out of the library, down the broad steps onto Hedley High Street. "It's the tomb in the legend. That's what she means. Now all we have to do is find it!" he said grimly as they set off to catch the bus home.

Chapter 6

"I think I'll go up to the Hall and say good-bye to Sophie." Kate announced at lunchtime next day. She liked the shy, quiet girl who read interesting books and who'd been having such a bad time of it lately. She was sorry that Francine Mason had decided to take her away, hidden tomb or no hidden tomb.

Todd didn't like goodbyes, and anyway Nick was more his friend than Sophie, and Nick was staying on at the house.

"Tell Jim and Nick I'll be up there later today," he said.

They'd agreed that the best way to solve the mystery of the tomb was to spend as much time working at the Hall as possible. However hard, however scary. They'd planned it on the back seat of the bus back from Hedley to Middleton. Lucy and Tez had both agreed to stay in close touch and help.

"We could try digging around in the garden," Todd had suggested. "There's broken walls and mounds of stuff all over the place. Maybe one is an entrance to where the body was buried!"

The others agreed; it was a good plan.

"I'll start out there, then!" Lucy decided.

Tez said he'd join her. "Two pairs of hands are better than one!" he announced. To himself, he had to admit he didn't fancy working inside those spooky walls, locked in with some old ghost. If he had to meet a ghost, he'd prefer to do it outside in the fresh air!

"If Jim Mason will let us!" Kate reminded them. She remembered how the cursed

brother in the story had begun to send everyone away and shut himself up alone in the
Hall. She half expected that to happen to Jim
now. Things would be even worse for him
once Francine and Sophie had packed up and
gone.

So when Kate went next day to see Sophie
off, she wasn't surprised that Jim was nowhere around. Todd's father had already
driven his Land Rover down from the farm
and was putting Francine and Sophie's bags
in the back. Francine stood, pale and quiet,
taking one last look at the Hall. One section of
roof was open to the air, where Jim had begun
to repair the timbers. Some outer walls were
partly rebuilt. But it was still just a shell. She
shook her head. "Hopeless," she sighed.
"Come on," she told Sophie as she climbed
into Mr Todd's vehicle.

Sophie gave Kate one of her sad smiles.

"Don't worry, we're going to help fix up the
old place!" Kate told her. "You'll soon all be

back together! The house will be as good as new!" she promised, trying to sound her cheerful self.

"It's not that," Sophie confessed. She cast a worried look towards the Land Rover. "It's my Dad that I'm worried about."

"Where is he now?" Kate whispered.

Sophie shook her head. "He was too upset to stay and wave us off, when he realized we were really going. He went off somewhere with Nick."

Kate nodded. "We'll do our best to look after him," she promised.

Sophie hesitated again. "He's still being weird," she said. It sounded awful, talking to other people about her father like this.

"Come on, Sophie!" Francine called from inside the car.

"OK!" She gave Kate one last, desperate message. "He's still going on about hearing voices everywhere! We tell him not to be daft, there are no voices. How could there be?"

"Sophie!" her mother called.

"Unless the house is haunted!" Sophie rushed on. She looked Kate straight in the eye. "Do you want to know what I think? I think this house has a ghost!" she said.

Kate stood there speechless.

"Do you believe in ghosts?" she gabbled. "I didn't before, but I do now!"

"Why?" Kate stammered. "What's been going on?" So much for not breathing a word about the legend, she thought. She wished she'd ignored the Todd family's advice to keep quiet. Poor Sophie had figured out the whole thing for herself in any case.

"There *are* voices in there at night. You can hear them!"

Kate looked sharply at the younger girl. "What kind of voices?"

"Two of them. They argue. And then things get bashed about. And then you go into the room and there's no one there!" Sophie said.

Mr Todd got down from the driver's seat and came grumbling across to where they stood. "Your mum's getting upset," he told Sophie. "You'd best come quickly." He looked firmly at Kate, then went back and started up the engine.

Sophie talked even quieter and faster. "My Dad hears these voices all the time, and he sees dark patches on the walls. I haven't seen them." She paused, wide eyed. "It's worst for him in the evenings." She grabbed Kate by the hand. "You will look after him for us, won't you?" she pleaded. Then she ran after Mr Todd and climbed up beside her mother.

The car door slammed shut. They waved at the vanishing Land Rover. Francine stared straight ahead, but Sophie turned briefly to wave back at them.

Kate watched the car disappear into the trees, then she turned to stare at the tall, silent grey house. I'm very scared! a small voice inside her admitted. Even in broad daylight it looks haunted to me now! Especially when you know the legend, when you've seen what happens to everyone who lives there!

Then she managed to get a grip on herself. "But it's up to us now!" she said firmly. She spotted Jim and Nick coming out of an old barn building across the yard at the back of the house. They dragged a bag of cement between them. Jim didn't look up to greet her. His face was ashen grey like the cement, his skin had a brittle, papery look.

Kate watched from a distance. "It's up to us, however scary!" she said again, gathering her courage.

But the stone walls of the Hall stood in shadow, its narrow windows like a prison. The house was determined to keep its secret entombed within those walls. The sun would never penetrate its damp and derelict rooms. The hidden tomb would never surrender itself to daylight, and the curse would remain!

* * *

Days went by and people in the village began to talk about Jim Mason. Mrs Hebden spoke to Mrs Todd; he'd gone very strange all of a sudden, no wonder his wife had taken the little girl away! "He doesn't speak, and he stamps around at all hours. Doesn't even have a civil word for Terry when he goes up with the groceries. Ignores his own lad too. Now that's who I feel really sorry for!" Mrs Hebden confided.

"Yes, and John said he felt for the wife in the end. She was in tears when she left, and he wasn't even there to wave them off!" Mrs Todd thought it was hard that a man should split his family over an old house. It was only a stack of stones after all. He could have packed up and admitted defeat. "He goes at it like a man obsessed!" she said darkly.

Then she thought better of it. "Still, I don't suppose he has much choice, after all. There's nowhere else for them to go, and he is trying to give his family a decent place to live," she said. "I just wouldn't like to be in his shoes, that's all."

Mrs Hebden agreed. "It's just as well the kids are still willing to lend a hand," Mrs Hebden said. "But I told our Terry not to get too involved. I want him home before dark these days. I don't want him hanging around there at night!"

Mrs Todd nodded. She'd already warned Todd and Kate, she said. But they were good kids and they'd set their minds on helping Jim Mason. "Perhaps they're better hearted than we are," she confessed. "Anyway, there's no stopping them now."

It was true, they had set their minds on being there and finding the hidden tomb. Nothing would put them off. Even though, when they went down to the Hall on the free days at the start of the summer holiday, Jim would stare fiercely at them, seeing them but not seeing them, muttering and pushing past with savage impatience. He was unshaven, hollow-eyed and wild in his actions. He climbed ladders which were unsafe until Nick came and steadied them. The roof was a nightmare of half-rotten beams and cracked stone slates, but still he clambered recklessly about.

"He's getting worse," Nick told Todd. They'd gone down to work and carry on the search for the whole day, a Sunday. There was a gloomy, hopeless feel about the place. "We're getting nowhere fast. He starts something and never finishes it. He just leaves a pile of rubble or another hole in the roof and goes off somewhere else. Then there'll always be something about the new place that scares the living daylights out of him, so he leaves a mess there and starts again." He sighed. "There's not a single room now that he hasn't wrecked!"

Todd glanced at Kate. Tez and Lucy were working out in the garden, uncovering an old pathway and a low wall at the edge of an overgrown terrace. But so far the mysterious mounds and ditches had revealed nothing of interest.

Up on the gallery they could hear loose stones falling from unfinished work on the roof. Kate stood next to Todd in a downstairs living-room, listening to Nick.

"Look there!" Nick pointed out of the open window after they heard footsteps run across the hallway and the sound of the main door being flung open. Jim Mason had rushed out into the garden. But then he stood still, head up like a fox listening, almost scenting the air, every sense alive. But they saw, felt, heard nothing!

"Mr Mason!" Tez dug his spade into the ground and approached him. "Would you like to see how we're getting on out here? We think we've just found what used to be a sunken pond!" He tried to sound cheerful, his usual self, though Nick's father was being so weird.

Jim Mason shook his head. "Do what you like!" he snarled. "Just as long as you stay out of my way!" He turned on his heel and strode back into the house.

Inside, he shot a look at Nick. "Tell them to stay out of the way!" he warned. "All of them!" He rubbed the palms of his hands up and down the sides of his jeans, and stood as if he was listening again. Then he rushed upstairs, past Kate and Todd, almost crashing against them in his hurry. He staggered on into one of the furthest rooms.

"Let's get on," Todd suggested in the midst of the strange silence. Better to be busy, better to concentrate on this search for the hidden tomb than to worry about what was happening to Jim Mason. He seized a hammer and chisel to begin chipping away at the crumbling old mortar on the wall Nick was working on.

Soon Kate and Nick joined him. The mortar fell easily away, it was so old. They made good progress. The room was an odd

shape, with archways and nooks leading nowhere. Kate thought of priestholes built into
these places hundreds of years ago; secret
hiding places for Catholics when the Protest-
ants hunted them down. It was like that here;
unexplained niches and hollows everywhere.

For some time they worked on in silence.
More and more odd-shaped stones appeared,
more and more unsolved puzzles.

"Hey, there's a face carved into this stone!"
Nick cried.

When Kate looked up she found it had
grown unexpectedly dark. She looked at her
watch and saw that it must be dusk. Evening
drew in. "Where's a face?" she asked.

Nick cleared stone dust from the small,
blurred shape. There was definitely a nose, two
eyes, a mouth, like an old carving in a church.

"Maybe it's a stonemason's mark?" Todd
suggested. "They all had a shape, a kind of
signature. So you'd know who'd built the
place."

"This must have been one of the important rooms then?" Kate noticed the long windows almost to floor level and some more elaborate carving around the fireplace. "Look, this little face is on some kind of arch, over the top of that doorway you thought you'd found," she said to Nick. "See? Two uprights, and now the arch overhead! Let's take away some more of the stones!"

Nick took a crowbar and began to lever away to make the hole bigger. They felt the excitement mount. The massive stones were hard to shift, and there was another layer beyond. This wall, like the rest, was many feet thick.

But then someone shouted a warning. A girl's voice, coming from outside. It was Lucy. "Kate! Todd! Nick!" She called them out.

"They must have found something!" Todd said. He dashed ahead of the other two.

"The tomb?" Kate said to Nick. "Maybe

they've found an entrance!" They followed quickly.

The smell of freshly dug earth greeted them. But no sealed, secret entrance, no tunnel into an underground vault.

Lucy and Tez's faces looked like white blurs in the gathering dusk. Lucy held up a hand in warning. "Listen!" she gasped. Tez stood beside her, silent and trembling.

At first they could hear nothing but the breeze in the dark trees. A rustling, whispering sound. But then the leaves turned to voices which uttered faint and unfamiliar words.

"Listen!" Lucy said again. "We both heard it!"

They strained to hear.

"Vile deed!" a voice whispered. "Oh vile deed!"

"What is it?" Kate felt Lucy come very close. Todd and the others froze.

"Shall I not be avenged!" the voice wailed.

"Shall I not visit this place and be avenged!"

They stood in the wilderness of a garden at dusk and heard voices float across the centuries.

"Thou shalt die!" another voice cried hoarsely. It seemed to come from the deepest shadows in the heart of the wood. It flew at them in the wind. "Thou shalt die and the house shall be mine hereafter!"

"Fond, rash man!" the first voice cried again. "Put up thy knife, for God will surely punish thee!"

"Brother, thou shalt die!" the second voice snarled. "And none will ever know of this deed!"

Kate gasped in fear and dread. Then the voices turned to sounds of brutal struggle. Bodies crashed and thudded around them. There was a horrifying cry and a loud moan. "I bleed!" someone cried. "Oh, brother, I bleed!"

"What shall we do?" Lucy gasped. She

looked fearfully into the darkening sky and back up at the house.

"Wait! I can still hear something!" Kate whispered.

The ghostly voices had ceased, though, "I bleed! I bleed!" echoed in their ears. Now other sounds came down through the ages.

There was a surge of waves, a lapping sound, and then a small tapping noise; a scraping and a tapping, and fainter still the first voice from beyond the grave. "Oh, wicked, miserable man!" it cried. "Save me! Repent and be forgiven! But seal me not inside this dreadful tomb!"

But the second, savage voice cried out again. "What you had is mine, and ever shall be! The Hall belongs to me and my children and my children's children! Resign thyself to death!"

"I bleed! I bleed!" came the faint, pleading voice.

At last the tapping ceased, and an eerie

silence followed. Kate looked around at the cluster of pale faces in the garden, witnesses to an ancient crime. Then a final surge overwhelmed them. A wind roared, a voice thundered. They cowered together in the tangle of thornbushes at the edge of the garden.

"Vengeance! Vengeance! Why, brother, I shall have vengeance!" A voice swelled around them. "I die by thy hand, but my spirit walks free of this hidden tomb! Whither wilt thou go, foolish man? For wherever thou goest, my spirit goes with thee. And it cries out for bloody vengeance! And thou shalt have blood on thy hands and my voice shall haunt thee forever! Yea, and thy children and thy children's children!"

The voice hissed through the trees and whirled about the clearing, in and out of the corners of the garden and the house. There was no escape. It froze the hearts of all listeners, and crept like ice over every inch of their flesh.

"And my voice will cry through the walls of this, my tomb! And my blood will cry out 'Murder!' in generations to come! Know that thou art cursed forever, until this deed be discovered!" The word 'forever' echoed, then there was silence, more deadly still. And a terrible suffocating cry from the dying man. He lost his battle for breath. "Bring it all down!" came the last choking cry. "Let it all come down!"

Chapter 7

The ghostly voice melted into the wind at last, but silence held them still as statues in the garden. Not a soul moved.

Great black rooks rose from the treetops and clattered clumsily through the purple sky. Their calls seemed to mock the group below.

Then there was a crashing, splintering noise from inside the house. Jim Mason staggered along the wooden gallery. He fell against the carved rails, he hit and kicked in every direction. Then he fell off balance and crashed downstairs. He picked himself up and thrust himself towards the old, arched doorway.

"No!" he screamed at invisible enemies. "Keep away from me! I didn't do it! I've done nothing wrong! Keep away!"

He stood outlined against the light in the hallway, his arms raised, the agony on his face lost in shadow.

"Dad!" Nick broke away from the group and began to run towards him.

"Nick, come back!" Todd lunged after him. He knew Jim Mason was blind and deaf to everything but the ghosts of the dead men.

But Nick ran on. "What is it? What can you see?" He grabbed at his father's shirt and pleaded with him.

Jim Mason fell back against the stone arch. "Terrible, terrible!" he moaned. "He buried him alive! He stabbed him and buried him alive!" His eyes were dark and blank. He pushed himself forward, crashed into Nick and stumbled a few steps down the weed strewn path. "But it wasn't me! I didn't do it!" he yelled at his invisible tormentor. The veins in his neck stood out, his eyes stared.

"What? Do what? We know you didn't murder anyone!" Nick tried to pull him back, but Jim gathered his strength and sent him flying towards Todd.

"Then what's this?" he moaned, clutching his hands to his head. "All these voices!" Confusion overwhelmed him.

Kate struggled to get near. She'd failed before. She'd run away from old Mr Mason and left him to die. This time she wouldn't do that. "They're not real! There's no one here!" she began.

Jim Mason seemed to hear what she said. He looked up at the sound of her voice. "But there's a man in there bleeding to death!" he cried. "They say it's my fault! They say I did it!" He shook his head frantically.

"Who?" Kate cried.

"The voices! Everyone!"

"They're not real!" she repeated, urging him. "You must believe it! There's nothing in there!"

"Yes!" he said, suddenly grabbing her arm and dragging her over the threshold back inside the Hall. "Listen! Look!"

She listened. The rush of rising water, the pounding of blood through veins, the suffocating, choking breath! She looked wildly round the stone floor, the broken stair rail, the beamed ceiling. Then at Jim Mason's crazy face; fear stricken, paralysed by the horror engulfing him.

Kate heard the voices whispering in her head. "Vile deed!" She stared at Jim Mason, frozen to the spot. "Thou shalt die!" said the hoarse voice with heart-stopping savagery. Jim rocked to and fro. "Stop them!" she cried. "Make them go away!" She put her hands over her ears. The voices were still there: "I bleed! I bleed!" Kate screamed.

The others clicked into action. They came running. But Jim Mason had already backed off from Kate. He crouched by the bottom of the stairs and grabbed one of the heavy demolition hammers stacked there. He went backwards up the stairs, slow and fumbling, still crouched like a cornered beast.

"Stop him!" Lucy gasped. But they were helpless. The curse held him fast. They watched him retreat upstairs.

"We haven't got long!" Kate said. "The end must be close, if we can all hear these voices! Remember the legend!" She heard Nick groan and felt him turn away in despair.

Jim had reached the gallery. He looked madly behind him down the long dark corridor, turned back and raised the hammer high above his head.

"Dad!" Nick pleaded. "Don't!"

But he brought the hammer crashing down against the stairs. Wood splintered and collapsed. He rained blows on the old steps and wrenched at them until they broke away. He stood at last on the landing, above a yawning gap as the staircase fell away. Then he edged backwards along the gallery and vanished into the gloom.

Sickened by the scene, Kate dragged herself outside. She was dizzy with fear as she headed for the yard. But when she got outside, she found that the voices had faded. The trees rustled but sent no message from the past. She stood, not daring to hope that the worst was over, then rinsed her face under the standing-tap to clear her head. The water felt clean and fresh.

"We can't get to him!" Todd had followed her out. "He's wrecked the stairs! What are we going to do?" He felt drained and helpless.

Kate felt the cold water rush over her hands. She splashed her face and looked back at the house. "Wait!" she said. She felt suddenly alert, as if someone had just shaken her awake from a nightmare. She stared at the kitchen window then at the light from the room next to it. "Is that room with the long windows the room where we were just working?" she asked.

Todd heard the note in her voice. It was urgent, almost electric. He followed her gaze. For a second he pictured Jim Mason up there in those unlit rooms, cut off, doomed and desperate. Then he concentrated. "Yes. It's next to the kitchen. That's the one!"

Kate breathed in sharply. "There's something odd!" she said. She approached the sheer stone outer wall and stood, head to one side.

"What?" Todd said. What was going on? Why was it so important?

She ignored him. She must think. "So inside here is the wall with the blocked-up doorway?" she said, pointing carefully. "Running at right angles to this outside wall. That's the wall that separates the living-room from the kitchen, then?"

Todd nodded. Suddenly the same thought struck him too. "I see!" he said. "Yes, that's weird!" He stood alongside Kate. "We're looking at a wall dividing two rooms that must be at least three metres thick!" he said.

"Well, it must be – look!" Kate peered in through the long window. "This living-room is much smaller than it should be! Or rather, that inside wall is much thicker than it needs to be, look!" She turned back to Todd.

"And the wall has a doorway which was meant to lead straight into the kitchen," he said. "Which it never did because it got bricked up for some reason!"

"Which means there could be a hollow gap somewhere between the kitchen and this living-room!" Kate cried. "No one in their right mind would deliberately build an inner wall three metres thick!"

"And!" Todd's mind raced alongside hers. "Come over here!" He dragged her to the smaller kitchen window and they both looked in. "That's the wall we're talking about on the other side, from the kitchen end!" He remembered it vividly; the one white wall which poor Oliver Mason was trying to paint. The one white wall in the grimy, terrible hole he called home. "He must have been trying to cover up the blood from the tomb!" he said.

Kate couldn't wait any longer. She led Todd down the side of the house and in through the front door. She beckoned the others into the kitchen after her. They all stood and stared at the wall, clean now and stripped of its old plaster.

"That's where he wrote the clue!" Todd said. "The same wall!"

"And it said 'TOMB'!" Kate said. "In big, scrawled letters. He wrote it and we couldn't see what he was trying to tell us!"

She took a chisel and hammer from the kitchen table and stepped across to the wall. Carefully she tapped the hammer and chisel along the width of the wall. Tap-tap, tap-tap.

Todd held his breath. It sounded normal; a dull, heavy thud beneath the metallic tap. Kate inched along. Suddenly the sound changed; sharper, with a faint echo at the end. "Stop!" he said.

They all stared at one another.

"It's hollow!" Lucy breathed. "Just back there! It's hollow! Where the door is meant to lead through from the other side!"

"It's the tomb!" Kate said. She said it and she knew it was true.

"Come on!" Nick said. "Let's find out, quick!"

He led them into the hallway and doubled back into the living-room next door. They began to work frantically on the half-demolished doorway.

They wrenched their arms almost out of their sockets, levering and pulling at heavy stones. Grazed and bruised, they scrabbled and heaved. They worked together to free the blocked doorway.

"Nearly!" Nick said. Dust and rubble piled up on every side. There was grit in his eyes and mouth. They worked grimly on.

"If we're right, what then?" Lucy whispered to Kate. The house was silent except for the demolition. Jim Mason hadn't come back along the torn and broken gallery. "What then?" she insisted.

Kate heaved at a huge stone to pull it free from the stone upright that formed part of the door frame. The wall was almost down. "I don't know! I just know we've found the tomb! And once we've found it, let's hope that's it, that the curse will be broken!"

"Will Jim Mason be OK?" Lucy said.

But Kate could only shake her head and pray. "I don't know. We've left it very late," she said.

Lucy came and lent her weight to the massive stone. It shifted and fell with a mighty crash.

"All I know is, the body of the first James

Mason is somewhere in here!" Kate said in a low voice.

"Nearly!" Nick said again. "But keep going! We've got to hurry!"

A last great stone fell away and they were through. Kate leaned forward across the rubble into the dark space. There was dead silence. Inside there was a small, clammy, dark hollow. Blackness. Silence. Black stone walls, a prison with no escape. A tomb.

"We need a torch!" she said faintly. And she began to claw her way up the rubble. She perched on the edge of blackness, ready to crawl in.

Chapter 8

Todd handed Kate the torch and she shone it down into the bottom of the tomb.

There seemed to be a drop of about a metre to the damp floor. She shone the yellow beam to left and right, but it was too weak to penetrate far into the darkness. "I'll have to jump down!" she whispered.

Todd felt his stomach tilt and lurch. "Are you sure you'll be able to get back up?" he asked.

Kate nodded. "The floor's only a little way

down, but I think there's a sort of corridor trapped between these two massive walls. I'll have to go down and take a closer look!" She handed the torch back to Todd and began to swing her legs into the opening. Gradually she eased herself down. She felt her way. Soon her feet touched solid ground.

Lucy's head appeared in the murky daylight above. "Can you breathe OK?" she asked.

Kate nodded. "No problem." It smelt musty, and the dark walls to either side felt icy cold, but fresh air had entered the ancient sealed cell as soon as they broke through the wall. "Pass me that torch again," she said to Todd.

"Are you all right?" he asked as he handed her the torch a second time. Beside and behind him, the others peered over the rim of the rubble down into the dark corridor. "Hang on, I'm coming in!" he said. He felt he had to be with Kate. He steeled himself and lowered his body to ground level beside her.

"Thanks!" she said. It did feel better to have Todd with her down in this terrible place. She knew only too well what they might find, and she didn't fancy being alone when it happened. Todd and she had been in this together from the start. Sure, they'd argued and seen some things differently, but in the end they were together. She shone the weak yellow beam along the rough surface of the far wall. "I wonder how far it stretches?" she whispered.

Todd glanced back at the anxious faces of Lucy, Nick and Tez outside, then along the secret corridor as far as the beam of light went. "All the length of the rooms above," he guessed. "Let's try this direction first!" He pointed left and they set off.

The corridor was just wide enough to walk normally, though their shoulders kept catching against jutting stones and their feet tripped on unseen rubble which littered the uneven floor. At every bump and stumble, Kate gasped and flashed the light up and down, around the walls. She caught Todd's face in its crazy spotlight. "What was that?" she cried out in a strange, muffled voice. The beam flashed down to their feet.

"A loose lump of stone!" Todd breathed. "Nothing!" Now they were here, he found himself hoping that 'Nothing' would always be the answer. An empty tomb! That was what he hoped for. Some chance! He gritted his teeth and waited for the inevitable gruesome discovery.

Slowly Kate inched forward. The darkness seemed to grow denser away from the opening. The walls seemed to be closing in. She shone the torch up their height and scanned the jagged surface. "It's like the Ghost Train!" she muttered, to relieve the tension.

"If only!" Todd replied. In the Ghost Train you rattled through quickly. The screams were recorded and the skeletons were fake. You came out into the fresh air laughing your head off. "Point the torch down on the ground. That's where we're likely to find what we're looking for," he said.

The beam swung across dusty cobwebs and ancient lumps of grey mortar. The stones at the base of the walls seemed to ooze dark, damp patches. But the ground was clear. Kate stretched out a hand and felt solid stone ahead. "We've reached the end," she whispered.

"You two OK down there?" Tez's muffled voice came through from a long way off.

"Fine!" Todd yelled. He took the torch from Kate as they shuffled to turn around in the narrow space. Now he was leading and she was behind. He shone the beam towards his feet and inched slowly back to where they'd begun. Kate followed. She kept one arm raised, the other touching Todd's shoulder.

"Find anything yet?" Lucy, Tez and Nick formed a triangle of faces peering down at the two of them from the jagged opening. Beyond them, the room looked murky. Lucy was the one who spoke up.

"Nothing." Todd ran the back of his hand across his eyes to clear the grit.

"Want someone to take over?" Tez offered, though it was the last thing he wanted to do. He didn't like closed-in spaces; they gave him the shakes and he went weak at the knees. But he had to offer.

Todd and Kate both shook their heads. "No, we're going to try the other direction," Kate said, "now that we're used to being down here!"

"Speak for yourself," Todd grumbled. But wild horses wouldn't drag him up now. He'd see this through to the bitter end.

"Rather you than me," Lucy admitted.

"Just hurry!" Nick urged. He was suffering the most. His father was hiding upstairs, driven crazy by ghosts. If this was the hidden tomb, then surely something should be happening by now. "There must be a body or something down there!" he said.

So Todd edged forwards into the blackness again. "This torch is useless!" he complained. It seemed to be growing fainter. He shook it impatiently.

"It's probably the batteries," Kate whispered. She picked her way around a jutting stone. Todd's face looked pale and distorted in the beam of light as he paused to examine the torch. He flicked it off. Pitch black! Then on again. The feeble yellow light returned. "Never mind, keep going!" she said.

So, slowly, dreading each second, they felt their way down the corridor.

"Wait!" Todd stumbled and Kate had to catch him to hold him back. His right foot had tangled in something soft. Not stone. Not cobwebs. He shone the torch down to his feet.

"It's a piece of cloth!" he said.

"Don't pick it up!" Kate warned. They crouched down for a closer look.

The fragment of brown fabric lay in the angle between the floor and the right hand wall. It had mouldered there untouched for years. But there was a row of cream coloured buttons along one edge which the torch easily picked out. Each button was as broad as a thumbnail, with a darker brown, rough surface. The whole scrap was probably nine or ten inches long.

"It's from a jacket or a waistcoat," Kate said. "Those buttons are made from horn."

Todd nodded. "There's something else underneath it," he said slowly. "Something shiny!" He looked sideways at Kate. "Shall I uncover it?"

"If you dare touch it!" she said.

Todd took a pencil out of his shirt pocket. "No need," he said. He poked the fabric to one side with the tip of the pencil.

"Hurry!" Kate warned. "This torch is fading fast!"

He held it close to the shiny object. It was small and round, fairly heavy, with beautiful flowing patterns carved into the surface. There were tiny hinges to one side. "It's a watch!" he said. Without thinking, he picked it out of the dirt and found the catch. It sprung open.

Kate stared at it in the palm of Todd's hand. Its creamy white face was painted with black roman numerals, untouched by the years of dirt. Its hands had stopped at seven thirty. "We'll keep it as evidence!" she said.

Todd closed it and slipped it into his shirt pocket. "You know what it means," he said. He'd have given anything for Kate to say, "Yes, it means there's a body here. It's James Mason. We know enough. Now let's go back!" But he knew her too well for that.

Kate nodded. "It means we were right; this is the hidden tomb. Now all we have to do is get him out of here!"

"Who?" He flashed the torch in her face, seized with panic.

"James Mason. We've got to get him out of here after all these years. We can't just leave him!"

"Why not! It won't make any difference!" Todd felt his heart race and pound. "It's only a dead body!" His mouth went dry, the nightmare charged all around him.

"It will make a difference to James Mason's ghost!" Kate insisted. " 'Thou art cursed forever until this deed be discovered!' Remember!" She repeated the words of the ghost in the garden. "He means until we get it out into the open!"

Todd groaned, but he knew she was right. You couldn't just go back with an old watch and prove a murder. Anyone could have dropped it there; a workman, anybody.

"Find anything yet?" Nick's voice yelled at them from the real world.

It jolted them onwards. "Yes!" Kate cried

out. "Just give us a few more seconds!" She kept tight hold of Todd as he shone the faltering torch and followed its faint beam.

His foot hit a metal object. It clattered against the solid wall ahead. The end of the corridor. A metallic clash.

"What was that?" Kate grabbed his shirt tight with both hands.

He bent forward.

Kate heard heavy movements blundering up from behind. She felt a hand flat against her own back. "Nick!" she cried, twisting round to see his shadowy face.

"Sorry. I didn't mean to scare you. I just couldn't wait up there any longer! Show me!" he whispered.

In silence Todd handed their latest discovery to Kate and she passed it on to Nick.

The metal felt freezing in the palm of his hand. It was long, heavy, pointed and sharp. "A dagger!" he whispered. His head began to spin.

"Oliver Mason must have sealed it up inside the tomb with the body!" Kate said. They studied the deadly, pointed blade for signs of blood, but though it was dull and covered in dirt, there was no bloodstain. "It would be the safest place to hide it!" she added.

The knife glowed dully in Nick's hand. He felt his fingers begin to curl around its handle, and he knew its dreadful fascination.

"Take it back!" Todd hissed. He felt crowded in, and he dreaded their next and final discovery.

Nick jerked into life. He took firm hold of the dagger and began to back down the narrow corridor. When he felt fresh air on his face, he turned and looked up at Tez and Lucy. He quickly handed Tez the evil thing and scrambled up through the hole.

"Is that it?" Tez asked. He passed the knife solemnly to Lucy. Then he helped to haul Nick the final stretch out of the tomb.

Nick nodded. It was like coming out of a dungeon, out of your own grave. He was too scared to speak.

"That's the murder weapon!" Lucy said. She felt the weight of it, the deadly point.

"Where are the others?" Tez had to shake Nick by the shoulder to make him answer.

"Still down there!" he gasped. "Still looking!"

"Have we gone as far as we can go?" Kate whispered to Todd.

He grunted and shook the wavering torch. It flickered out, then glowed, dimmer than ever. "A dead end," he said.

"Then shine the torch on the ground again." She shivered in the clammy, dark place. "Go on, Todd, shine it down!"

Reluctantly he pointed the torch into the last shadowy corners.

"There!" Kate said.

He froze the beam.

They stared down at what they most dreaded. There was the dome of a skull, the deep eye sockets, the grinning mouth. It glimmered dirty yellow in the faint torch-light. Beside it there was a crumbling heap of bones, all over the place, unrecognizable. There, a fragment of leather with a buckle. There, the sole of a shoe turning to dust.

Todd gasped and shuddered. He turned away.

Kate imagined the man's last moments – trapped, bleeding to death, suffocating. Oliver Mason had heaved the last stone into place and cemented it in. "Oh, brother, I bleed!" James had cried. He'd breathed his last, beating his fists against the cruel walls. Stabbed and covered in blood inside this airless tomb. "But seal me not inside this dreadful tomb!" Darkness. Death.

Full of pity, Kate leaned beyond Todd. He was pressed back against the wall, struggling not to yell out in fright. She picked up the brittle, light skull and gently held it between both hands. Todd recoiled further. "Come on," she whispered. "We found what we came for!"

Without caring that the torch had flickered and died, she trod surely back, the skull between her steady hands. When she felt the fresh, sweet air above she looked up and saw the same circle of faces. "It was all true!" she told them. "The legend was true. Oliver Mason murdered his poor brother and buried him here in this hidden tomb!"

As she spoke, there was a great rush of air. It seemed to come crashing out of the hollow tomb itself, and with such force that the skull flew from her hands as she held it up for them all to see. It fell and shattered. The doors flew open to right and left. The windows shook and rattled. It grew. Todd came stumbling down the narrow gap after Kate, feeling the wind whip through his hair, almost lifting him off his feet and hurling his bruised body against the wall. Kate caught hold of him and made a human chain with those outside the tomb. Straining against the force of the mysterious wind, Kate and Todd were pulled clear.

But the mighty wind whirled through the house. Window panes rattled and shattered. Glass splintered to the ground. The wind began to escape.

Then they heard a voice above it, rising to a shout, a scream. "Vengeance! Vengeance!" it roared in every dark corner, up the broken staircase, out through the open rafters. "And thou shalt have blood on thy hands and my voice shall haunt thee forever!"

There was a horrific swell, a tide beating at the walls of the house. A pounding, invisible tide. "Yea, and thy children! And thy children's children!"

It was as if the voice and the wind sucked them free of the shaking, shattered shell of a house, out into the dark tangle of the garden.

They didn't resist. The wind blew and they held themselves upright.

"Oh, stop!" Lucy cried. She whirled against Tez and hid her face. For she'd looked back at the house and the horror was never-ending.

There was a figure standing in a shattered window; high up, arms braced against the stone frame. He yelled above the wind.

"It's Nick's father!" Tez shouted. He pointed to where the moonlight caught the figure in its white glow. Still the wind battered everything in its path.

"Make it stop! Stop it!" Nick pleaded with Kate. "You must know how to make it stop!"

But the skull lay shattered on the stone floor and chaos was let loose. "I don't!" she cried. "I don't know what's happening!"

"Listen! What's he saying?" Nick yelled.

They strained to hear Jim Mason's wild words.

He pointed. He leaned forward, horrified,

on the edge of death. "Vengeance!" he cried.

And then some great shadow seemed to pass over the house; a great, glistening black stain. It rose up the walls in the moonlight, flooding the Hall. It reached the high window where Jim Mason sat and cried out.

"Why, brother, I shall have vengeance!"

The shadow swept over the rooftop.

Jim groaned and slumped forward. He swayed with the dark tide.

"He'll fall!" Nick cried.

"We can't reach him!" Lucy gasped. "We can't rescue him!"

Kate stood in the garden below, sick at heart. They'd freed the spirit from its secret grave. They'd tried to break the curse of Middleton Hall.

But the vengeful ghost of James Mason had been let loose on the world and he would destroy everything. No, they couldn't save Jim. They were helpless. The wind tore at her clothes and hair. She turned to Nick.

He stared at his hands. He heard his father moan, but his eyes were fixed on nothing. The voices gripped him in their power and tormented him. He held them up to his face. "They're here! Can you hear them? They'll haunt us for ever." He looked up at her in terror. "Get them away from us!" he pleaded.

Chapter 9

"What have I done?" Kate cried. She ran and searched for Todd. She was hopeless, helpless. She went from one dark figure to the next. They stood still and cold as stone, staring up at the swaying man.

Lucy shook her head. She couldn't speak. Her eyes filled with hot, stinging tears. So she hid her face against Tez's shoulder, unable to look. They shivered and tried to find shelter from the wind. The shadow was evil, Kate knew. It drenched everything in its dark power.

Todd stood with his back to the house. He

looked out at the trees of Middleton Woods. If Jim Mason fell, he didn't want to see it. Kate found him standing in the gateway, his face set into a blank stare. "Todd, what's happening? What have I done?" she cried.

He raised himself from his daze and glanced at Kate's terrified face. "No, not you. You didn't do anything," he told her. "You did your best!"

"But it's worse! We made it worse! Now that we've let the ghost loose, the curse is falling on everyone! On Jim, on Nick, on everyone!" she wailed.

Todd spun round. "Nick?"

"Yes. Now he can't get rid of the voices!" She pointed to where Nick crouched, desperate to block out the dreadful noise.

"Can you hear them?" Todd demanded. He began to run towards Nick.

"Not now!" She ran with him. "But this is terrible!" The wind seemed to sigh and groan.

Todd grabbed hold of Nick and pulled him

to his feet. "Nick, listen!" He wanted to shake and smack him, wake him up, break the curse.

Nick stared back with dark, blank eyes, then slumped to the ground again. He was like his father, raging in another world, trapped inside a vision of murder and endless revenge.

Todd held Nick's hands in front of his face. His fingers were like black prison bars. His eyes glinted white. "Listen, they'll go away, just hang on! You hear me?" he shouted savagely.

Nick stared through his hands and moaned. "No! No!"

"He can't hear!" Kate cried. She looked up at the window to see Jim's dark figure slumped and tilting forward, almost off balance. He was slipping into unconsciousness. Now, any second now, he would fall!

Then the wind seemed to ease. The doors in the house no longer heaved and battered at their hinges. They swung to and fro. The black shadow flickered and shifted.

"It's stopping!" Tez told Lucy. "Feel it!"

The wind sighed and groaned. A voice swirled around them. "Forever!" it whispered and echoed. "Ever! Ever! Ever!" The shadow drifted. It sank from the rooftop. Chimney stacks glowed an eerie pale grey in the moonlight. It sank again, the tide had begun to turn. Empty windows came into view. The shadow fell and fell. "Until this deed is discovered!" the voice said.

"Murder!" it whispered. It was a sigh, it grew fainter. "Oh, brother! Murder!" The voice sank with the shadow down the front of the house. Jim Mason was bathed in silver light. His head hung forward; close, close to the edge. But his eyes opened. They saw him brace himself and recognize his danger.

The shadow sank past the arched doorway. It fell on the dark earth and swept back through the tangled garden. Lucy and Tez felt the sickening, clammy darkness lift and leave them in the light. They stood upright and breathed again as the shadow swept by. They looked up at the clear stars.

"Oh, brother!" the voice sighed in the trees of Middleton Woods. It was a faint cry of sorrow.

"It's going away!" Kate whispered. There were tears in her eyes as she knelt down beside Nick and Todd.

Nick slumped forward, taking his weight on his hands. Todd put an arm around his shoulders. When he looked up, his eyes had cleared.

"It's gone!" Kate whispered again. Nick could hear her. He'd come back!

He nodded. The garden shimmered in pure light. The moon was full and shining on the house and garden. "You set it free!" he told her. She joined their embrace. It was over. There would be no more voices.

The others ran across to join them. Suddenly everyone talked at once, mad with excitement. They saw Jim struggle to his feet and heard him shout down, "Just what's going on here?" He sounded dazed but normal. He was looking round to see how he could climb back off the window ledge to safety.

"Dad, we're down here!" Nick scrambled to his feet. He held up his hands and waved them in the air. "Listen, they've gone! No more voices. They've gone for good!" he yelled.

The trees of Middleton Woods sighed, the water of the lake rippled and lapped at the pebbled shore.

"The curse is broken. I can feel it in my bones!" Nick shouted out in his delight.

Todd grinned. He slapped Kate's back. "Well done, you broke the curse!" he said.

"*We* broke it!" She looked around the circle of relieved, wondering faces.

Then Todd had a thought. He put his hand in his shirt pocket and clasped his fingers around the watch they'd found in the tomb. It seemed like years ago. "You should have this," he told Nick. He handed the warm, smooth, silver object to him. "It belongs to your family. And I feel we've got to settle things. They've got to be absolutely right!" he said.

Nick took the watch and stared down at it without speaking.

"And let poor James Mason rest in peace," Kate agreed. She smiled warmly at Todd.

"What happened to the dagger?" Tez asked. If people outside wanted to know the truth about what had happened all those years ago, the dagger would be the proof.

Lucy frowned. "I must have dropped it back there when that wind started up. It scared the living daylights out of me. It must be still inside the house!"

Everyone hesitated. No one wanted to go back in just yet. There was the smashed skull, as well as the dagger. It would be like stepping back into a grave.

Nick glanced up at the empty windows of the upper storey. "It's OK. I'll give Dad a shout. He can bring it out with him. He must be making his way down right now." He strode towards the house to yell the message.

But a new noise made him stop in his tracks. Not loud at first, but it froze him to the spot. Everyone stopped and stared at the Hall.

A creaking, grinding noise. Things shifted. An unseen door banged. Then there was a moment of dreadful silence.

"What is it?" Tez asked. They couldn't see anything. But the grinding, splitting noise began again.

They looked up. Things happened in slow motion. An unbelievable second frozen in time, when one of the great stone chimney-stacks swayed. It tilted sideways, it held steady, then the whole thing split and fell. Stones dropped through the air, smashed on to the roof, bounced and fell on to the ground.

"Stand back!" Todd yelled a warning.

Nick didn't move. His father was in there. He watched the roof sag and crack right down the middle.

There was a huge roar of stone slates as it collapsed. A ripple, like a giant pack of cards, as the slates flipped and fell. A dense cloud of dust. The timbers creaked and split, and as they fell, they smashed against walls and ceilings, pounding at them until they too began to crumble.

"The whole place is caving in!" Tez yelled. He began to grab people and drag them back. Stones thudded into the grass where they stood.

"Oh no!" Lucy gasped and held on to Kate. An outside wall had begun to crack. A stone lintel across the top of a window collapsed. The noise deafened them.

And Kate remembered the last terrible words the ghost had uttered. It came to her with a whisper out of the treetops and it rose to a mighty roar. James Mason's final threat: "Bring it all down! Let it all come down!"

Rafters cracked, walls tumbled like thunder. There was another mighty rumble of stones sliding to the ground. An avalanche into the yard. And everything seen only as a blur through a storm cloud of ancient dust.

"Dad!" Nick yelled above the noise. He saw a shape struggle into a window frame at the far end of the house. He must have run back along the gallery away from falling masonry. But he was still up there, trapped.

Jim felt the house crumbling around him. He looked down at the figures frantically waving and shouting in the garden, far too close to this death-trap. "Get back!" he yelled down at them. He thought he saw Nick, and someone struggling to pull him clear of the falling stones. Jim glanced back into the hell hole behind him. That way there was no escape.

"He'll have to jump!" Lucy cried. It was a

daunting height, a sheer drop of about twelve metres.

"And break his back!" Kate said. She shook her head. "We can't get to him this way. We'll have to reach him from inside!"

"It's useless!" Tez had run as close as he dare to peer inside the main doorway. Through the dust he saw a mountain of rubble, walls caving in everywhere. "That wall we knocked through to get into the tomb must have held the whole house up!"

Lucy nodded. "We didn't know what we were doing when we bashed that hole. We must have weakened the wall holding a main part of the roof up!" She watched in dismay as more stones tumbled.

"Get back!" Jim yelled again. He waved his arms. "Get back, everyone! You'll get your-selves killed!"

"What about you?" Nick screamed up at him.

"Never mind! Stand clear, I'm telling you!"

Jim clutched the window frame as part of the floor behind him began to creak and split. A great hole yawned in one corner of the room. The noise beat all clear thoughts out of his brain. He clung onto the window frame for dear life. "Stand clear! Stand clear!" he yelled.

But Nick looked up. Dizzy with fear and deaf to reason, he began to run towards the house.

Chapter 10

Nick dodged the falling stones. He used his jacket as a shield against the dust, pulling it across his mouth as a kind of mask. And he raced right into the collapsing building.

"Bring it all down!" Kate heard again. It echoed inside her head. The whole thing would fall. She saw Todd begin to run in after Nick. Was he trying to stop him?

But Todd wrenched a short ladder from its place against the front wall. It was still in one piece. He yelled an instruction. Nick stopped and grabbed the other end of the ladder. Together they disappeared inside the house.

Kate's heart fluttered and almost stopped. It was crazy to go in there! Who knew which wall would go next? The roof had fallen in and now there was nothing to stop the whole thing cracking and splitting apart.

But she couldn't stand by and watch. She took all her courage into her hands and ran into the great dust cloud. Into the heart of chaos.

"Kate!" Lucy's voice cried out. It drifted up into the night.

Kate ignored her and ran on.

"Dad!" Nick's voice got lost in the confusion inside the Hall. There was no reply.

Choking, almost blinded, Todd yelled out, "He can't hear you! Here, put the ladder up against the gallery. We'll have to climb up and get him down!"

They scrambled through the rubble. The dust was so thick you couldn't see where the next avalanche of stone was going to happen.

Nick stumbled and fell. The metal ladder clattered down. They tried once more to raise it up against the gallery platform. Kate was beside them now, grazed and bleeding. She helped set the ladder firm on the stone floor.

"I'll go up!" Nick gasped.

There was no way to argue, so Todd and Kate held the ladder steady, heads down, mouths clamped shut. Still the debris showered down on them.

Nick climbed the ladder and hauled himself across on to the wooden platform. Boards were shattered, the whole floor tilted under a weight of broken stones at the far end. But he made his way along at reckless speed. He yelled for his father. "Dad, this way!"

Jim crouched, looking down at the dark, sheer drop. If it came to it, he would jump. Seconds ticked by. A gable at this side of the house gave a sinister crack. Soon that wall would go too. He prayed that his part of the building could stand until help arrived.

Then he heard Nick's voice from deep inside the Hall. "Dad, this way!"

Jim groaned. He should have jumped earlier and risked it. Then Nick wouldn't have had to try this crazy heroic trick. "Stay there!" he yelled. He dropped down from the window ledge back inside the wrecked room.

Nick appeared in the doorway, coated in grey dust.

"Watch the holes!" Jim yelled. "Stay where you are! I'm coming!"

"We've got a ladder. We can get you down!" Nick told him. He grasped his father's arm. "Down here. You've got to come this way!"

"I told you to stay clear!" Jim shouted at him. "Not risk your own neck!" But he grabbed his son by the shoulders and hugged him.

The gable end cracked wider. They stepped quickly on to the battered gallery floor and made their way along it.

"Keep your back to the wall!" Nick told

him. "There's stuff still dropping from the roof!" It clattered on to the platform, ripping chunks from it. At last they reached the ladder.

"You first!" Jim ordered.

Nick swung himself onto the ladder.

Todd and Kate down below felt it take his weight. They heard two voices.

"Hurry up!" Kate urged. She could hardly see anything when she looked up; just a shape beginning to appear.

Then an earthquake. A huge, shuddering collapse of wall, gallery, ladder, rubble. Everything fell in.

Nick yelled out loud and slid the length of the ladder. Someone grabbed him from below. Using their arms to shield their heads, mouths full of dirt, eyes weeping soot and grime, they stumbled, staggered, clambered towards what had once been the front door.

Lucy and Tez stood helpless. The whole house had gone; Jim's window, the gable, the inside walls; everything! But two figures came out, clawing their way through the rubble.

"Who's that?" Lucy breathed. They rushed forward to help.

Todd was blinded with filth. "Where's Kate?" he wanted to know. His face was smeared with dirt and tears. He gasped for breath.

"Still inside, with your dad and Nick!" Tez told them in a quiet, empty voice. How could anyone survive a moment more of this? They stood waiting for the dust cloud to settle.

Jim had felt the gallery smash downwards. He'd covered his head with both hands. Kate had felt the ladder buckle and slide out of her grip. She heard nothing but a massive grinding and smashing. She felt a section of wooden boards slide on top of her. She sheltered under there as the stones rained down. They thudded against her wooden shield, threatening to crack it apart.

Another body slid through the rubble. Jim Mason caught a glimpse of Kate cowering in her shelter and wrenched her out as a huge section of wall began to topple on to it. They were both free and in one piece. Kate's sloping shelter shattered like matchwood.

Now they could only crawl through the rubble inch by inch. It was impossible to see a way through. Blindly, grasping each other tight, they tried to struggle free.

"It's no good, we're at a dead end!" Jim shouted. He groped at an upright surface in front of them. "We'll have to crawl back some other way!" They'd found the only wall left standing and it blocked their way!

"No, wait!" Kate crawled up beside Jim and felt the thick wall. She tried to get her bearings. Where were they? Which way should they try now? Then she stopped. It was possible! It was just possible! More stones and beams crashed around them. She dived forward, dragging Jim with her.

"What the..." Jim cried out in sudden shock.

They fell a short way. Then Kate crawled ahead down a rough narrow corridor. It was one person wide, dark and damp. The walls still stood because they were massive. Some kind of ceiling kept stones from falling and choking up the passage. So they crawled a few feet into safety.

Middleton Hall crashed down around them and James Mason's final curse took its course. "Let it all come down!" Stones thundered, the house was rubble, but Jim and Kate crouched together and waited for it all to end.

Jim caught his breath. His whole body was bruised but not broken. "Where are we?" he gasped.

Kate choked out her incredible reply. "We're in the hidden tomb!" she said.

"It seemed to me to be the right thing." Jim Mason sat in his shirt sleeves, resting his arms on the table. "From what you tell me about the legend, no one deserved to keep the

Hall, right from the start!"

"James Mason made sure of that!" Kate agreed. "That was one thorough curse!" And he must be one satisfied ghost, she thought.

She could laugh about it now. The rich green leaves of the oaks and chestnuts lifted and turned in the breeze. Three days had passed since Middleton Hall had crashed to the ground. Kate and Jim would never forget the long wait in the dark until the house had finally fallen and the rescuers, with ropes and pickaxes, could come climbing over the rubble, hoping against hope to find someone alive.

"It was like getting survivors out of an earthquake!" Todd told them. "We thought we'd need stretchers and ambulances at least!"

"The tomb saved us!" Kate reminded them. "Strange, that." She thought for a moment. Perhaps that had even been part of the plan too? If you thought that these

things were meant to happen in a certain way
... it was fate! What else had led them,
crawling and choking, to the only bit of
shelter left standing at the end of it all? She
shrugged.

"Anyway, justice was done," Jim said,
serious for a moment. They looked across the
sunny space at a mass of fallen stones and
timber.

"You're not saying you're actually glad it
fell down?" Lucy said. She was sitting on the
caravan steps, learning how to chew the sweet
end of a blade of grass. Todd had shown her
how to pick it by sliding it free of its sheath.

Jim smiled. "In a way, yes." Nick was at the
table beside him, sitting in the open air,
studying a plan which they had spread open
on the table for inspection. "Who needs a
haunted house?" he said with a shrug and a
grin.

"Especially when we can start over," Nick
agreed, "with a nice modern place." The plan

showed a house with big windows, wide doors, patios. A house open to the sun.

"And when we have neighbours like the Todds here who lend us a caravan while we get on with rebuilding," Jim said, "and a whole gang of willing helpers to get us under-way!" He grinned again at Kate and the others. "What more can we ask?"

They all sat smiling back at him; Kate, Todd, Lucy, Tez and Nick. The summer was nearly over. They'd see the foundations dug, and then they'd be back at school, back in routine. Then the walls would begin to go up again, using the old stone.

"Will you still call it Middleton Hall?" Kate asked.

Nick pulled a face. "No way! Mum said she wouldn't stay here and live in it if we called it that!"

"It's quite true!" Francine stuck her head out of the caravan window. She'd driven through the middle of the night with Sophie to be here when she'd heard the Hall had fallen down. Her sister had brought them back to Middleton to find a ruined house and a husband restored to his old self.

"We may be using the old site and the old stone, but we're not keeping the old name!" She smiled, but she was very firm. "This is a time for a clean break with the past!" she said.

The caravan, tucked away on level ground under the old apple trees, caught the late afternoon sun. They happily lazed the time away.

Then Sophie came into view. She picked her way between the fallen timbers of the old house, bending to pick up a heavy stone and carry it across. "Look at this!" she called out.

Curious, Kate strolled over. She smiled, then examined the stone in Sophie's arms. With her fingertips she traced an outline carved into the surface; an oval shape, two eyes, a nose, a mouth. It was a face. "It's the mason's mark," she told Sophie.

Sophie looked up and shivered. "The Masons' mark?" she echoed.

Kate smiled. "Not the Mason family, but mason as in stonemason," she explained. "Well, both really!" And she told Sophie parts of the old story; how Oliver and James had been the masons who'd built all the old farms around here, how their family had been stonemasons way back as far as records went.

The two of them strolled over to the table with the stone and set it down.

Francine came out and traced the shapes on its surface. She looked up at the calm sky and across to the ruined house. The Mason family; it was their mark.

"I suppose we could use this above the new doorway," she said. She felt herself soften. After all, the past couldn't harm them now. "What do you think, Kate?"

Kate looked round the whole big group. The quaint carved face would look down on all who entered the new house. They would always remember the old. She heard a breeze lift and sigh through the branches. She nodded. "Good idea," she said.

Goosebumps

by R.L. Stine

Reader beware, you're in for a scare!

These terrifying tales will send shivers up your spine . . .

Available now:

The Babysitters Club

Need a babysitter? Then call the Babysitters Club. Kristy Thomas and her friends are all experienced sitters. They can tackle any job from rampaging toddlers to a pandemonium of pets. To find out all about them, read on!

Our favourite Babysitters are detectives too! Don't miss the new series of Babysitters Club Mysteries:

Available now:

No 1: Stacey and the Missing Ring
When Stacey's accused of stealing a valuable ring from a new family she's been sitting for, she's devastated – Stacey is *not* a thief!

No 2: Beware, Dawn!
Just *who* is the mysterious "Mr X" who's been sending threatening notes to Dawn and phoning her while she's babysitting, *alone*?

No 3: Mallory and the Ghost Cat
Mallory thinks she's solved the mystery of the spooky cat cries coming from the Craine's attic. But Mallory can *still* hear crying. Will Mallory find the *real* ghost of a cat this time?

No 4: Kristy and the Missing Child
When little Jake Kuhn goes missing, Kristy can't stop thinking about it. Kristy makes up her mind. She *must* find Jake Kuhn . . . wherever he is!

No 5: Mary Anne and the Secret in the Attic
Mary Anne is curious about her mother, who died when she was just a baby. Whilst rooting around in her creepy old attic Mary Anne comes across a secret she never knew . . .

No 6: The Mystery at Claudia's House
Just what is going on? Who has been ransacking Claudia's room and borrowing her make-up and clothes? Something strange is happening at Claudia's house and the Babysitters are determined to solve the mystery . . .

No 7: Dawn and the Disappearing Dogs

Dawn decides to try her hand at *pet*sitting for a change, and feels terrible when one of her charges just . . . disappears. But when other dogs in the neighbourhood go missing, the Babysitters know that someone is up to no good . . .

No 8: Jessi and the Jewel Thieves

Jessi is thrilled to be taking a trip to see Quint in New York, and thinks that nothing could be more exciting. But when they overhear a conversation between jewel thieves, she knows that the adventure has only just begun . . .

No 9: Kristy and the Haunted Mansion

Travelling home from a game, Kristy and her all-star baseball team are stranded when a huge storm blows up. The bridges collapse, and the only place they can stay looks – haunted . . .

No 10: Stacey and the Mystery Money

When Stacey gets caught with a fake banknote, the Babysitters are astounded. Can *counterfeiters* really have come to Stoneybrook? The Babysitters have to solve the mystery, clear Stacey's name *and* save their reputation . . .

Look out for:

Hippo Fantasy

Lose yourself in a whole new world, a world where anything is possible – from wizards and dragons, to time travel and new civilizations . . . Gripping, thrilling, scary and funny by turns, these Hippo Fantasy titles will hold you captivated to the very last page.

The Night of Wishes
Michael Ende (author of *The Neverending Story*)

Malcolm and the Cloudstealer
Douglas Hill

The Wednesday Wizard
Sherryl Jordan

Ratspell
Paddy Mounter

Rowan of Rin
Emily Rodda

The Practical Princess
Jay Williams

If you like animals, then you'll love
Hippo Animal Stories!

Look out for:

Animal Rescue by Bette Paul

Tessa finds life in the country *so* different from life in
the town. Will she ever be accepted? But everything
changes when she meets Nora and Ned who run the
village animal sanctuary, and becomes involved in a
struggle to save the badgers of Delves Wood
from destruction . . .

Thunderfoot by Deborah van der Beek

Mel Whitby has always loved horses, and when she
comes across an enormous but neglected horse in a
railway field, she desperately wants to take care of it.
But little does she know that taking care of
Thunderfoot will change her life forever . . .

A Foxcub Named Freedom
by Brenda Jobling

A vixen lies seriously injured in the undergrowth. Her
young son comes to her for comfort and warmth. The
cub wants to help his mother to safety, but it is
impossible. The vixen, sensing danger, nudges him
away, caring nothing for herself – only for
his freedom . . .